Primo Levi was born in ~~Turin in 1919~~, and graduated with honours in chemistry shortly before the racial laws prohibited Jews from taking academic degrees. In 1943 he joined a partisan group in northern Italy and was arrested and transported to Auschwitz. It was his knowledge as a chemist which saved his life. His camp was liberated in 1945, and Primo Levi was then sent with other Italians to White Russia. After his return to Italy, he continued to work as a chemist until his retirement in 1975. Primo Levi died in April 1987.

Apart from *The Wrench* Primo Levi's other works are *If This Is A Man* (*Se questo è un uomo*; 1958), *The Truce* (*La Tregua*; 1963, winner of the Premio Campiello), *Natural Stories* (*Storie Naturali*; 1967, winner of the Premio Bagutta), *A Structural Defect* (*Vizio di Forma*; 1971), *The Periodic Table* (*Il Sistema Periodico*; 1975, winner of the Premio Prato), *Moments of Reprieve* (*Lilit e altri racconti*; 1981) and *If Not Now, When?* (*Se Non Ora, Quando?*; 1982, winner of the Premio Campiello and the Viareggio prize). In addition, he has written a volume of poetry, *Shema*, and a collection of short stories, *The Drowned and the Saved* (*I Sommersi e i Salvati*; 1986). *The Wrench* (*La Chiave a Stella*) was first published in 1978.

270 6243

THE
WRENCH

TRANSLATED FROM THE ITALIAN BY WILLIAM WEAVER

PRIMO
LEVI

SPHERE BOOKS LTD

Penguin Books Ltd, 27 Wrights Lane, London W8 5TZ (Publishing and Editorial)
and Harmondsworth, Middlesex, England (Distribution and Warehouse)
Viking Penguin Inc., 40 West 23rd Street, New York, New York 10010, USA
Penguin Books Australia Ltd, Ringwood, Victoria, Australia
Penguin Books Canada Ltd, 2801 John Street, Markham, Ontario, Canada L3R 1B4
Penguin Books (NZ) Ltd, 182–190 Wairau Road, Auckland 10, New Zealand

First published in Great Britain by Michael Joseph Ltd 1987
Published in Abacus by Sphere Books Ltd 1987

Originally published in Italian as *La Chiave a Stella* 1978
First published in English in the USA as *The Monkey's Wrench*
by Simon and Schuster Inc. 1986

Italian text © Giulio Einaudi editore s.p.a. 1978
Translation © Summit Books, A division of Simon and Schuster Inc. 1986
All rights reserved

. . . though this knave came somewhat saucily into the world . . .
there was good sport at his making.

—*King Lear*, act 1, scene 1

"WITH MALICE AFORETHOUGHT"

NO, NO, I CAN'T tell you everything. Either I tell you about the country, or else I tell you what happened. But, in your place, I'd pick what happened, because it's a good story. Then, if you really want to write it down, you can work on it, grind it, hone it, deburr it, hammer it into shape, and you'll have a story. And, even if I am younger than you, a lot of stories have happened to me. Maybe you'll guess the country anyway, and that'll be all right. But if I tell you where it was, I'll get into trouble: the people there are nice, but they're kind of touchy."

I had known Faussone for only two or three evenings. We ran into each other by chance in the mess, the dining hall for foreign visitors in a very remote factory where my job as a paint chemist had taken me. We were the only two Italians. He had been there three months, but he had stayed in those parts on other occasions, so he could manage pretty well with the language, in addition to the four or five he already spoke, making plenty of mistakes, but fluently. He's about thirty-five, tall, thin, almost bald, tanned, always clean-shaven. His face is serious, rather immobile, not very expressive. He's not a great story-teller. On the contrary, he's somewhat monotonous, playing things down, elliptical, as if he were afraid of seeming to exaggerate. But often he lets himself go, and then, unconsciously, he does exaggerate. His vocabulary is limited, and he frequently expresses himself through clichés that to him seem original and clever. If his listener doesn't smile, Faussone repeats the cliché, as if he were talking to a simpleton.

". . . like I told you, it's no accident that I'm in this line of work, going from one construction site to another, to all the factories and ports of the world: it's what I wanted. All kids dream of going into the jungle or the desert or Malaya, and I also had those dreams, only I like to have my dreams come true; otherwise they're like some disease you carry around with you all your life, or like the scar of an operation that, whenever the weather turns damp, it starts aching again. There were two ways for me: I could wait till I got rich and then be a tourist, or else I could be a rigger. So I became a rigger. There're other ways, too, of course: being a smuggler, you might say, and like that. But they're not for me. I like to visit foreign countries, but I'm a regular guy, all the same. By now it's become such a habit that if I had to settle down quietly, I'd get sick. If you ask me, the world is beautiful because it's all different."

He looked at me for a moment, with unusually inexpressive eyes, then he patiently repeated: "A man stays home, and maybe he's peaceful and all, but it's like sucking an iron tit. The world is beautiful because it's all different. So, like I was saying, I've seen plenty of places and had all sorts of adventures, but the craziest story was what happened to me this past year, in that country. I can't tell you where it is, but I can tell you it's a long way from here and also from our home, and here we're suffering the cold, but down there nine months out of twelve it's hot as hell, and the other three months the wind blows. I was there to work in the port, but down there it isn't like it is with us: the port doesn't belong to the government, it belongs to a family, and the head of the family is the one who owns everything. Before I started working, I had to go call on him, all dressed up in a coat and tie, have something to eat, make conversation, smoke, without any hurry. Imagine! When we have every minute budgeted. What I mean is, we cost real money; we're proud of it. That head of the family was a kind of half-and-half character, half modern and half old-fashioned; he was wearing a beautiful white shirt, the kind that don't have to be ironed, but when he came into the house he took off his shoes, and he made me take mine off, too. He spoke English better than the English (not that it takes much), but he wouldn't let me see the women of the house. He was a kind of progressive slave owner; and—can you believe it?— he had his picture framed and hung in all the offices and even in the warehouses, like he was Jesus Christ or something. But the whole country is pretty much like that: there are donkeys and telexes, airports that make Caselle back in Turin look sick, but usually you can get to a place quickest on horseback. They have more nightclubs than bakeries, but you see people walking around the streets with trachoma.

"I don't mind telling you that rigging a crane is a great job, and a bridge crane even more; but they're not jobs just anybody can do. They take somebody who knows the tricks, who can run things, men like us; the others, the helpers, you pick up on the spot. That's where the surprises come in. In that port I'm talking about, the union situation is a mess, too. You know: a country where if you steal something they chop off your hand in the square, left hand or right, depending on how much you stole, and maybe an ear, too, but all with anesthetic and topflight surgeons, who can stop the bleeding in a second. No, I'm not making this up, and anybody who starts slander about the important families, they cut out his tongue, and no ifs or buts.

"Well, along with all this they have some pretty tough organizations, and you have to deal with them: all the workers down there carry a transistor around with them, like it was a good-luck piece, and if the radio says there's a strike, everything comes to a halt, and not one of them dares lift a finger. For that matter, if he tried to, he'd likely get a knife in him, maybe not right there and then but two or three days later;

or else a beam falls on his head, or he drinks a coffee and keels over on the spot. I wouldn't like to live there, but I'm glad I've been, because some things, if you don't see them, you don't believe them.

"Well, like I was telling you, I was down there to erect a crane on the dock, one of those big bastards with a telescope arm and a fantastic bridge, a span of forty meters, and a one hundred forty-horsepower lifting motor. Jesus, what a machine. Tomorrow night remind me to show you the photos. When I finished putting it up, and we ran the test, and it seemed to walk in the sky, smooth as silk, I felt like they'd made me a duke, and I bought drinks for everybody. No, not wine: that slop of theirs that they call *cumfàn* and tastes like mold, but it cools you off and it's good for you. But I'm getting ahead of myself. This job wasn't so simple; not for any technical reason, all that part went fine right from the first bolt. No, it was a kind of atmosphere you could feel, like heaviness in the air just before the storm breaks. People muttering together at the street corners, making signs and faces at one another that I couldn't understand; every now and then a wall newspaper would appear, and everybody would crowd around to read it or have it read to them; and I would be left alone, perched on the top of the scaffolding like a dumb bird.

"Then the storm broke. One day I saw them calling one another, with gestures and whistles: they all left, and then, since I couldn't do anything by myself, I came down the tower, too, and went to take a peek at their meeting. It was in a half-built shed: at the end they had set up a kind of stage, with beams and planks, and, one after the other, they came up on the stage and spoke. I don't understand their language much, but I could tell they were mad, like somebody had wronged them. At a certain point this older character came up; he seemed to be a local chief. He also sounded very sure of what he was saying; he spoke calmly, with lots of authority, not yelling like the others, and he didn't need to, because while he stood there they all shut up. He gave them a calm speech, and they all looked convinced; at the end he asked a question, and they all raised their hands, shouting I don't know what. When he asked who was opposed, not a single hand went up. Then the old man called up a boy from the front row and gave him an order. The boy raced off, went to the tool store, and came back in a minute, carrying one of the photographs of the boss and a book.

"Beside me there was an inspector, a local guy, but he spoke English, and we were sort of friendly, because it's always a good idea to stand in with inspectors."

Faussone had just finished a generous helping of roast beef, but he called the waitress and made her bring him another portion. I was more interested in his story than in his maxims, but he inevitably repeated himself: "It's the same the whole world over, and that's the truth: every saint wants his candle. I had given that inspector a fishing rod, because you want to stand in with inspectors. So he explained it to me. It was crazy: for a long time the workers had been asking for the kitchen to cook them food according to their religion. The boss gave himself airs of being modern, though in the end he was a bigot of some other religion. That country has so many religions that you can't keep them straight. Anyway, he had the head of personnel tell them that they could either take the mess hall the way it was or they wouldn't have any mess hall. There had been two or three strikes, and the boss hadn't yielded an inch, because business was slow anyhow. Then there was the idea of getting physical with him, if you follow me. To get even."

"What do you mean by getting physical?"

Faussone patiently explained that it was like putting a curse on someone, giving him the evil eye, a spell. "Maybe not to kill him. On the contrary, that time there they surely didn't want him to die, because his little brother was worse than he was. They only wanted to throw a scare into him, you know, a sudden illness, an accident, just to make him change his mind, and to show him, too, that they knew how to make their demands felt.

"Then the old man took a knife and unscrewed the frame of the picture. He looked like a real expert in that kind of thing. He opened the book, closed his eyes, and put his finger on a page. Then he opened his eyes again and read something I didn't understand, and neither did the inspector. He took the picture, rolled it up, and pressed it hard with his fingers. He had somebody bring him a screwdriver, heated it till it was red-hot over a spirit-lamp, and stuck it inside the flattened roll. He unrolled the photo and held it up, and everybody clapped. There were six scorched holes: one on the forehead, one near the right eye, one at the corner of the mouth. The other three were in the background, not touching the face.

"Then the old man put the photo back in the frame, just like it was, all wrinkled and perforated, and the kid ran off to hang it in its regular place, and they all went back to work.

"Well, in late April the boss took sick. They didn't come out and say it, but the rumor went around right away, you know how these things are. He seemed really bad from the start; no, there wasn't anything wrong with his face: the story is weird enough without that. The family wanted to put him on the plane and take him to Switzerland, but they didn't have time. It was something in his blood, and ten days later he was dead. And he was a sturdy guy, I tell you, never been sick before, always shooting around the world in his plane, and between planes always chasing women, or gambling from dusk to sunrise.

"The family charged the workers with murder, or rather 'homicide with malice aforethought'; I was told that's how they call it down there. They have courts, you understand, but they're the kind it's best to stay clear of. They don't have just one code of laws; they have three, and they pick this one or that one, depending on which works best for the strong side or who pays the most. The family, like I said, insisted it had been murder: there was the intention to kill him, the actions to make him die, and death. The defense lawyer said the actions hadn't been murderous: at most, they would have given him a bad rash, or a boil, or pimples. He said that if the workers had cut that picture in half or had burned it with gasoline, then it would have been serious. Because that's how a spell works, it seems: a hole causes a hole, a cut causes a cut, and so on. It makes us laugh a bit, but they all believe in it, including the judges, and even the defense lawyers."

"How did the trial end?"

"You're kidding. It's still going on, and it'll go on for God knows how long yet. In that country trials never end. But that inspector I mentioned promised to let me know, and if you want, I'll let you know, too, since you're interested in this story."

THE WAITRESS came, bringing the spectacular portion of cheese Faussone had ordered. She was about forty, bent and skinny, her lank hair greased with God knows what, and her poor little face seemed like a scared goat's. She gave Faussone a long look, and he looked back at her with a show of indifference. When she went off, he said: "She looks kind of like the jack of clubs, poor thing. But what the hell, you have to take what life offers."

He indicated the cheese with his chin and, with scant enthusiasm, asked me if I would like some. He then went at it greedily and, between chews, he continued: "As you know, here, the girls department is kind of poorly stocked. You have to take what life offers. I mean what the factory offers."

CLOISTERED

WELL, IT'S UNBELIEVABLE. I can understand how you wanted to write about it. Yes, I knew something myself; my father told me. He was in Germany, too, in a different situation. In any case, I'll tell you this: I've never taken on any jobs in Germany; it's a place I've never liked. And I can get along in lots of languages, even with a smattering of Arabic and Japanese; but I don't know a word of German. One of these days I'll tell you about my father, the story of how he was a prisoner of war; but it's not like yours, it's more something to laugh at. And I've never been in prison either, because nowadays, to end up in jail, you really have to do something big. All the same—can you believe it?—I had a job once that for me was worse than prison, and if I ever really did have to go to jail, I don't think I would last two days. I'd bash my head against the walls, or else I'd die of heart failure, like nightingales and swallows when you try to keep them in a cage. And don't get the idea this happened to me in some far-off country. No, it was a stone's throw from home, a place where on a clear day, if there's a wind, you can see

Superga and the Mole Antonelliana. But, around those parts, you don't get clean air all that often.

"They called me, and some others, for a job that was nothing out of the ordinary, really: normal site, normal difficulty. I've told you the place; or rather, I didn't tell you the exact spot, because the fact is that it's kind of a professional secret with us, too, like doctors and priests when you confess. As far as the difficulty went, it was nothing but a truss tower, about thirty meters high, six by five at the base, and I even had plenty of help. It was autumn, neither hot nor cold. In other words, you could hardly call it a job; it was a job that was a rest from other jobs, a chance to catch a breath of home air. And I needed that, because I had just had a nasty time with a bridge in India, and that's a story, too, that I'll have to tell you one of these days.

"The design was nothing out of the ordinary, either: all structural steel, L and T beams, no tricky welding, standard grill flooring. And the idea was to assemble the tower on its side, so there was never any need to climb more than six meters, or even to hitch myself up. In the end they'd bring up a crane to set it erect. What the thing was for, at first, was something I hadn't given any thought. From the drawings I could see it was going to support a fairly complicated chemical plant, with big and little tubes, like columns, heat exchangers, and all sorts of pipes. All they told me was that it was a distillation plant, to extract an acid from the waste water . . . because otherwise . . ."

Unconsciously, unintentionally, I must have assumed a particularly interested expression, because Faussone broke off and then, in a half-amazed, half-irked tone, said, "Sooner or later, unless it's a secret, you're going to tell me what line of business you're in and what you're doing in these parts." Then he went on with his story.

"But even if I didn't know the whole story, I still enjoyed seeing it grow, day by day; and it was like seeing a baby grow: I mean a baby that isn't yet born, when it's still inside its mama. Of course, this was a funny baby because it weighed about sixty tons, just the framework, but it didn't grow all anyhow, like a weed; it grew up neat and precise, like it was in the drawings, so when we fitted the ladders from one level to another, and they were fairly complicated, they fit right off without any cutting or welding, and this is a real satisfaction, like when they made the Frejus tunnel, and it took thirteen years, but then the Italian hole and the French hole met, without any error, not even twenty centimeters, so afterward they raised that monument, the one that's all black, in Piazza Statuto, with the flying lady on top.

"Like I said, I wasn't alone on this job, though with a job like that, if they gave me three months and a pair of smart helpers, I would manage pretty well on my own. There were four or five of us, because the client was in a hurry and wanted the tower erected in three weeks, maximum. Nobody put me in charge of the team, but right from the first day it came natural for me to give the orders, because I had the most experience, which with us is the only thing that counts; we don't have chevrons on our sleeve. I didn't talk much with this client—he was always in a hurry and so was I—but we hit it off right away, because he was one of those men who know their business and don't give themselves any airs and can command without ever saying one word louder than the other, and they don't make a fuss about what they're paying you, and if you make a mistake they don't get all that mad, and when they make a mistake they think it over and apologize to you. He came from our parts, a little guy like you, only a bit younger.

"When all thirty meters of the tower were finished, it took up the whole yard, and it looked clumsy, a little ridiculous, the way all things meant to stand erect look when they're lying down. I mean, it was sad, like a tree that's been chopped down, and we quickly called the cranes, to set it up. It took two of them, the tower was so long, and they hooked it at the two ends and slowly carried it to its reinforced-concrete base, which was all finished, with its moorings ready; and one of the two cranes, with a telescope arm, was to pull it up and then settle it in place. Everything went fine; the trip from the yard to the warehouses went without a hitch; then, to take it around the corner of the warehouses, we had to knock down a fair amount of masonry, but nothing serious. When the bottom of the frame was on the base, we sent the smaller crane home, and the big one stretched its arm out all the way, with the tower dangling from it, and little by little it straightened up. And even for me—and I've seen my share of cranes—it was a beautiful sight, also because you could hear the engine purring calmly, as if to say for him, too, it was child's play. It lowered its burden right on the spot, with the holes right on the bolts, and we tightened them, had a drink, and went off. But the client came running after me; he said he had the greatest respect for me, and the toughest part of the job remained to be done; he asked me if I had other commitments and if I knew how to weld stainless steel. And, to make a long story short, since I didn't have anything else lined up and I liked the man, and also the job, he hired me as chief rigger for all the distillation tubes and for the work and service pipelines. Service means where they send the cooling water, the steam, the compressed air, and so on; the work pipes are where the acids to be processed pass. That's what they're called.

"There were four tubes: three little ones and one big one; and the big one was plenty big. But the rigging wasn't hard. It was simply a vertical pipe of stainless steel, thirty meters high: in other words, as high as the tower that, in fact, was meant to support it. And a meter in diameter. It had been brought up in four sections, so it was a matter of making three joins, one flanged and two edge-welded, a run on the inside and one on the outside, because the plate was ten millimeters thick. For the inside run, I would have to have myself lowered from the top of the tube in a kind of cage, like a parrot's cage, hanging from a rope; and this wasn't much fun, but it only took me a few minutes. Then, when I began with the pipelines, I thought I'd go crazy, because I'm really only a journeyman rigger, and I'd never seen a job so complicated. There were more than three hundred pipes, of every diameter, from a quarter-inch to ten inches, and every length, with three, four, five bends, and not all of them at a right angle. And one pipe was actually of titanium, which I didn't even know existed, and it made me sweat blood. That was the one the most concentrated acid passed through. All these pipes connected the big column with the smaller ones and with the exchangers, but the design was so complicated that even if I studied it in the morning, by nightfall I'd already forgotten it. And for that matter, I never understood in what way the whole plant was meant to work.

"Most of the pipes were of stainless, and you know that's great stuff, but it won't give. I mean, when it's cold, it just doesn't have any give. . . . Didn't you know that? Sorry, I thought you people learned these things in school. It doesn't give, and if you heat it, then it's not all that stainless after. In other words, there was a lot of fitting, pulling, filing, and then taking apart. When nobody was looking, I'd even give it a few licks with my hammer, because your hammer can fix everything, and in fact at the Lancia works they used to call it 'the engineer.' Well, when we finished with the pipes, it looked like Tarzan's jungle, and it wasn't easy to get through. Then the insulators came to do their insulating and the painters to do their painting, and what with one thing and another a month went by.

"One day I was right at the top of the tower with my box-end wrench to check if the bolts were all tight, and I see the client coming up, kind of slow, because thirty meters is like a house eight stories high. He had a little brush, a piece of paper, and a sly look, and he started collecting the dust from the head plate of the tube I had finished rigging the month before. I eyed him suspiciously, and I said to myself: He's here looking for trouble. But he wasn't. A little later, he called me and showed me the paper; he had brushed a bit of gray dust into it. 'You know what this is?' he asked me. 'Dust,' I answered. 'Yes, but dust from roads and houses doesn't come all the way up here. This dust comes from the stars.'

"I thought he was making fun of me, but then we climbed down, and with a magnifying glass he showed me that the dust was all little round balls, and he showed me how a magnet attracted them. They were iron, in other words. And he explained that they were falling stars that had come to the end of their fall; if you climb up fairly high in a clean, isolated place, you always find some, provided there's no slope and the rain doesn't wash them away. You won't believe it, and neither did I at first; but with my work I often happen to be up high in places like that, and I've seen that dust is always there, and the more the years go by, the more there is, so it's like a clock. I mean like one of those hourglasses you use for boiling eggs; and I've collected some of that dust in every part of the world, and I keep it in a box at home, I mean at my aunts' home, because I don't have a place of my own. If we're in Turin together one day I'll show you, and when you think about it, it's kind of sad, those shooting stars that look like the comet over a Christmas crib, you see them and you make a wish, and then they fall down and cool off and become little balls, two-tenths of a millimeter. But don't let me get off the track.

"I was telling you: when the job was over, that tower looked like a forest; and it also looked like those diagrams you see in doctors' waiting rooms, The Human Body, one with all the muscles, one with the bones, one with the nerves, and one with the guts. Actually, it didn't have muscles, because there wasn't really anything that moved, but it had all the rest, and I was the one who had fitted the veins and the guts. Gut number one, I mean the stomach and the intestine, was the big tube I mentioned before. We filled it with water up to the top, and we dumped two truckloads of Raschig rings into the water: porcelain rings as thick as your fist. The water was there to make sure the rings sank down gently, without breaking, and once the water had been drained away, the rings were to act like a maze, so the mixture of water and acid that entered the tube, halfway down, would have time to separate well: the acid should run out from the bottom, and the water would turn into steam and escape from the top, then condense again in an exchanger, and end up I don't know where. Like I said, I never rightly understood all those chemical things. The point was that those rings shouldn't break; they had to settle slowly, one on top of the others, until they filled the tube up to the top. Dropping those rings was a sweet job: we hoisted them up by the bucket with an electric hoist, and we slid them into the water nice and slow, and it was like when kids make sand pies on the beach and the grownups say, Be careful or you'll get all wet. And sure enough, I did get all wet, but it was hot so I actually enjoyed it. It took us almost two days. There were the smaller tubes, and they had to be filled with rings, too; what those ones were for I honestly couldn't say, but it took only another two or three hours. Then I said good-bye, went by the office to collect my pay, and since I had a week's vacation due, I went up to Val di Lanzo to fish for trout.

"When I take a vacation I never leave an address behind, be-cause I know very well what happens then; and, in fact, I come home and find my aunts scared to death, with a telegram from the client in their hands, because for them, poor women, a telegram is something to get all het up over: 'Signor Faus-sone please contact us immediately.' Well, what could I do? I contacted them, which means I called them on the phone, but 'contacted' sounds grander. And from the tone of the man's voice I realized first thing that something was wrong. He sounded like a person who's calling for an ambulance but doesn't want to show how upset he is; he wants to maintain his style. I was to drop everything and come straight up, be-cause there was an important meeting. I tried to find out what kind of meeting and what I had to do with it, but nothing do-ing: he just insisted I should come right away, and he sounded like he was ready to cry.

"So I go, and I find all hell's broken loose. He, the client, had a face like somebody who's been out on the tiles all night, but, instead, he'd been sitting up with the plant, which was acting funny. The night before, obviously, he had let fear get the best of him, like when you have somebody sick in the fam-ily and you can't figure out what the trouble is, then you lose your head and call six or seven doctors when it would really be better to call just one, a good one. He had sent for the de-signer; the constructor of the tubes; two electricians, who glared at each other like cat and dog; his chemist, who was also on vacation but had been made to leave his address; and a guy with a potbelly and a red beard, who talked like a school-book and it wasn't clear what his connection was, and later we found out that he was a friend, a lawyer, but I think the client hadn't sent for him as a lawyer, but just to keep his courage up. All these people were standing there at the foot of the tube, looking up, and they paced back and forth, tramping on one another's feet, and trying to calm down the client. And they were all talking balls; the fact is that the tube was also talking, and it was exactly like when somebody is running a fever and is raving, but seeing that he's maybe about to die, everybody takes him seriously.

"Sick. Yes, that tube was really sick: anybody could see that, and I could even see it myself, though I was no expert, and the client had sent for me only because I had put the rings in. It had like an attack every five minutes. You could hear a sort of hum, faint and calm at first; then it became louder and irregular, like a big animal that's short of breath. The tube began to vibrate, and after a little while the whole structure went into resonance, and it seemed an earthquake was coming on, and then everybody acted like nothing was happening: one guy would fix his shoelace, another would light a cigarette, but they all moved off a way. Then you would hear a sound like the beat of a bass drum, but muffled, like it had come from underground, a sound of backwash, I mean like gravel spilling out, then nothing, only the same hum as before. All this happened every five minutes, regular as a clock; and I can tell you this because even if I didn't have much to do with it, I and the designer were the only ones who managed to stay fairly calm and look at things without losing our head. And the longer I stood there, the more I had the impression that I had a kind of sick child on my hands. Maybe it was because I had seen it grow up and had even gone down inside to do the welding; or maybe because it was moaning like that, meaninglessly, like a kid that still can't talk but you can see he's sick; or maybe it was even because I felt like a doctor: when he's treating somebody who's sick inside, first he puts his ear to the patient's back, then he taps him all over, and sticks in the thermometer. And that's exactly what the designer and I were doing.

"If you put your ear to that metal sheeting, when the attack was going full blast, it was really scary: you could hear a big noise of guts in upheaval, and my own personal guts came close to moving, too, but I controlled them for the sake of my dignity. And as for the thermometer, obviously it wasn't like ordinary thermometers for taking your temperature, the ones they stick in your mouth or vice versa. It was a multiple thermometer, with lots of bimetals in all the strategic points of the setup, a dial and about thirty buttons, for choosing the point where you wanted to read the temperature. In other words, it was an intelligent instrument, but since the center of the big tube, the one that was sick, was really the heart of the whole system, at that point there was also a special thermocouple, which operated a thermograph: you know, one of those nibs that writes the curve of the temperature on a roll of graph paper. Well, that was even more scary, because you could see the whole clinical history, from the first evening, when they made the plant operational.

"You could see the start, I mean the line that set out from twenty degrees and, in two or three hours, went up to eighty, then leveled off, a nice and even stretch, for about twenty hours. Then came what looked like a shudder, very slight—you could hardly see it—that lasted only five minutes; and after that, a whole series of shudders, more and more violent, and all exactly five minutes long. The last ones, actually, those of the night before, weren't shudders at all; they were waves that bounced ten or twelve degrees, rising sharply then plunging headlong, and we caught one of those waves then, the designer and I, and could see the line going up just as all that commotion went on around us, and then it made a nasty dive the minute you heard that drumbeat and the noise of the gravel. The designer was young but he knew his business, and he told me that the other guy had called him in Milan the night before because he wanted authorization to shut everything down, but the designer was uneasy and had preferred to jump into his car and come up himself because the question of shutting down wasn't all that simple and he was afraid the client would make a mess, but now there was nothing else to do. So he had done it himself, and in half an hour everything stopped, you heard a great silence, the curve zoomed down like a plane landing, and it seemed to me that the whole installation heaved a sigh of relief, like when they give a sick person morphine and he falls asleep and for a while he's out of pain.

"I kept saying that I had nothing to do with any of this, but the client made us all sit around a table, so each could speak his piece. To tell the truth, at the beginning I didn't dare speak my piece, but there was one thing I did want to say, because I was the one who had dropped in the rings, and since I have a pretty keen ear I had heard that the sound of stirring guts was the same sound as when we emptied the rings from the buckets into the column: a backwash, like when a dump truck comes and unloads gravel; it hums and goes up and up until, all of a sudden, the gravel starts to slide and it comes down like an avalanche. Finally I told this idea of mine in a whisper to the designer, and he stood up and repeated it with fine words like the idea had been his, and according to him the tube's ailment was a case of flooding. You know how some people are: if they want to make themselves important, they'll grab any opportunity. So the tube was flooding and it had to be opened, drained, and looked into.

"No sooner said than done. Everybody began to talk about flooding, except the lawyer, who laughed to himself like an idiot and said something, aside, to the client; maybe he was already thinking about a lawsuit. And everybody looked at yours truly, as if it was already agreed that the man to save the situation was me; and I must say that, at heart, I wasn't sorry, partly because of curiosity and also partly because that moaning tube that collected stardust on top and was shitting itself . . . right, I hadn't told you this, but it was obviously building up pressure, because at the peak of each wave, from the gasket of the bottom manhole you could see a kind of brown sludge come out, dripping down over the base. Well, I felt honestly sorry for it, like it was a person in pain, who can't talk. Sorry, and irritated, the way you get with sick people, and even when you're not fond of them you end up helping to cure them, at least so they'll stop moaning.

"I won't tell you how much trouble it was to take a look inside. It turned out that there was two tons of acid in there that cost money, and anyhow you couldn't empty it into the sewer because it would've polluted the whole area; and since it was acid, you couldn't pour it into any old tank: It would have to be stainless steel, and the pump also had to be acid-proof, because the stuff had to be drained upstream, since there wasn't enough of a slope to do it by gravity. But all together, we pulled off the job, drained the acid, purged the tube with steam so it wouldn't stink so much, and then we waited for it to cool down.

"At this point, like it or not, I was on stage. There were three manholes: one at the top of the tube, one toward the middle, and one at the bottom. You know they're called like that because they are those round holes that a man can get through; they also have them on steam engines, but the name doesn't mean that a man can get through them all that comfortably, because the diameter is only fifty centimeters, and I know some guys with a bit of a pot who either couldn't get through or else got stuck. But, as you can see for yourself, I've never had any problems in that area. I followed the designer's instructions and I began to unscrew the top manhole slowly, to make sure no rings came out. I shift the big cover, I stick a finger inside, then my whole hand. Nothing. The logical thought was that the rings had all settled a little farther down. I take off the cover, and all I see is blackness. They pass me a flashlight. I put my head in, and I still see black: no rings, like I had only dreamed about dropping them inside there. All I could see was a well that looked like it didn't have a bottom; and only when my eyes got used to the darkness, I saw a kind of whitish glow way down that you could barely glimpse. We lowered a weight attached to some string, and it struck bottom at twenty-three meters: our thirty meters of rings had shrunk to seven.

"There was a lot of talk and argument, and in the end we got to the bottom of it all—and that's not a figure of speech—because the rings were actually ground up and all on the bottom. You can imagine the story. I told you, the rings were ceramic and were fragile, and that's why we used water as a shock absorber when we dropped them in. Obviously some of them had begun to break and the bits made a layer at the bottom of the column; so the steam had to force its way and would suddenly break through the layer, and that would shatter more rings, and so on. When you figured it out—and the designer did the figuring on the basis of the rings' dimensions—there couldn't have been very many of them left intact. And, sure enough, I opened the middle manhole and found empty space. I opened the lowest one, and I saw a sandy cake and some little gray stones, and that was all that was left of the load of rings: a cake packed so hard that it didn't even move when I pulled aside the cover.

"It was all over but the funeral. I've seen quite a few of these funerals, when you have to get rid of a mistake, hide it, and it stinks like a corpse, and if you leave it there to rot it's like a constant sermon, or rather, it's like a court sentence, a reminder to everybody who had anything to do with it: 'Never forget, you were responsible for this screw-up.' It's no accident that the ones most anxious to hold the funeral are the very ones who feel most responsible, and this time it was the designer, who came over to me, acting nonchalant and saying it just needed a good washing out with water, then all that muck would go away in a minute, and we'd put in some new rings, stainless steel, at his expense, of course. When it came to the washing and the funeral, the client agreed, but when he heard the mention of more rings, the man turned into a wild animal: the designer ought to raise an altar to the Madonna in thanks for not being sued, but no more rings. He had to figure out something better and be quick about it, too, because the client had already lost a week's production.

"None of this was any fault of mine, but seeing all those downcast people around me, I felt sad myself, partly because the weather had turned bleak, and it looked more like winter than fall. Then we soon saw that the job wouldn't be so fast: obviously that muck, I mean the broken rings, was rough fragments, and they had got all stuck together; in fact, the water we hosed over them came out at the bottom as clear as it went in, and all those dregs wouldn't budge. The client started saying that maybe if somebody was lowered down inside with a shovel, but he was just talking, not looking anybody in the eye and in such a timid voice that it was obvious he had no faith in what he was saying. We tried different ways, but finally we saw that the best method was to send the water in from the bottom, the old system when somebody's constipated. We screwed the hose to the drain of the tube, we turned it full on; for a while we didn't hear a thing, then there was like a great sob, and the stuff began to stir and come out, like mud, from the manhole; and I felt like I was a doctor, or rather a vet, because at this point instead of a baby that sick tube began to seem like one of those prehistoric animals that were tall as a house and then all died out God knows why. Maybe it was constipation.

"But, unless I'm mistaken, I started this story in a different direction, and then it got out of hand. I started telling you about prison, and about this job that was worse than prison. Obviously if I had known in advance the effect it was going to have on me, I would never have accepted such a job, but you know how it is: a man learns late to say no to a job, and to tell you the truth, I still haven't learned it today, so you can imagine me then, when I was younger, and they offered me a figure so high that I was already thinking of a two-week vacation with my girlfriend; and besides, you have to remember that I've always liked to step forward when all the others are stepping back, and I still do, and they had figured out the kind of guy I am. They flattered me and said how they could never find another rigger like me, and they had such confidence in me, and this work involved real responsibility and such. Well, I said yes, but it was because I didn't realize.

"The fact is that the designer, smart as he was, had made a king-size mistake. I caught on from the talk I was hearing and also from his face. Apparently in that sort of tube rings, ceramic or any other material were no good, because they were an obstacle to the steam, and the only thing was to fix plates in there, pierced disks, in other words: stainless steel, one every half-meter, about fifty in all. . . . Ah, you know those plates? You do? But you surely don't know how they're rigged; or maybe you do have an idea, but you can't know what it's like to rig them. That's only normal, after all; a man drives a car, but he doesn't ever think of the work that's condensed in it; or else he does some figuring on one of those calculators you can slip in your pocket, and at first it seems a miracle and then he gets used to it and it seems natural. For that matter, it seems natural to me that when I decide to raise this hand here, my hand goes up, but it's all a matter of habit. That's why I enjoy telling about my jobs: it's because so many people have no idea. But let's get back to the plates.

"Every plate is divided in two, like two half-moons that fit one into the other. They have to be divided like that, because if they were all one piece it would be too hard to mount them, or maybe impossible. Each plate is set on eight little brackets welded to the wall of the tube, and that was my job, mounting the brackets, starting from the bottom. You work your way up, welding all around, until you reach the level of your shoulder, no higher because it gets too tiring, as you know. Then you set the first plate on the first circle of brackets, you climb on to it with rubber-soled shoes, and about half a meter higher, you weld another circle of brackets. From above, the assistant lowers another pair of half-moons, you fit them, a section at a time, under your feet. And so on. A ring of brackets, then a plate, another ring, another plate, all the way to the top. But the top was thirty meters high.

"Right. I did the scribing without any trouble, but when I was two or three meters from the bottom, I began to feel funny. At first I thought it was the fumes from the electrode, though there was good ventilation; or maybe my mask, because if you do welding for so many hours in a row, you have to cover your whole face, otherwise you scorch your skin, and it all peels off. But then it got worse and worse; I felt like I had a weight here at the top of the stomach, and my throat was tight like a kid's when he wants to cry. Most of all, I felt my head swim: I remembered lots of things I had long forgotten, that sister of my grandmother who had become a cloistered nun—'She who passes beyond this door, dead or alive, comes out no more'—and the stories they told in the village, about the man they put in the coffin and buried and he wasn't dead, and at night in the graveyard he hammered with his fists to get out. That pipe, too, seemed to be getting narrower all the time and it was suffocating me, like a rat in a snake's belly; and I looked up and saw the top, far, far above, to be reached by half-meter steps, one at a time; and I felt a great longing to get myself pulled out, but I didn't give in because after all the fuss they had made over me I didn't want to look like a fool.

"Well, it took me two days, but I stuck with it, and I got to the top. All the same, I don't mind telling you that since then, every so often, I get that trapped rat sensation: most of all in elevators. It isn't likely to happen to me on the job, because now I leave all the inside jobs to the other guys; and I consider myself lucky because in my line most of the time you're out in the open air, and maybe you have to contend with heat, cold, rain, dizziness, but there are no problems of being cloistered. I've never been back to see that tube, not even from the outside; and I keep clear of all tubes, pipes, passages; and in the papers when I see stories about people being held for ransom, I don't even read them. There you are, it's stupid, and I know it's stupid, but I've never been able to be the way I was before. In school they taught me concave and convex; well, I've become a convex rigger, and concave jobs are not for me any more. But if you wouldn't tell this to anybody else, I'd appreciate it."

THE HELPER

OH, FOR GOD'S SAKE! There's no comparison.
Me, I've never complained about my fate, and if I did complain, I'd be a fool, because I chose it myself: I wanted to see foreign places, work hard, not be ashamed of the money I earn. And what I wanted is what I got. Obviously there are pros and cons, and you being a family man, you know that very well. In fact, a man can't have a family this way, or even any friends. Or maybe you do make some friends, but they last as long as the job lasts: three months, four, at most six, then you catch the plane. . . . By the way, here they call a plane the *samolyot:* did you know that? It's always seemed a fine word to me, it makes me think of *siulòt,* what we call onions back home. Yes, it reminds me of *siulòt,* and of *scimmiotti,* monkeys. But I'm straying from my story again. About catching the plane? I was saying it's goodbye for good then. Either you don't care, and that means they weren't real friends; or else they were, and you're sorry. And with girls it's the same, worse really, because you can't do without, and one time or another, sure as hell, you get caught."

Faussone had invited me for a cup of tea in his room. It was monastic, and completely identical to mine, even in the details: same lampshade, same cover on the bed, same wallpaper, washbasin (and his dripped exactly the way mine did), the radio without a knob on the shelf, the bootjack, even the cobweb over the corner of the door. But I had been living in mine for only a few days, and he had been here three months: he had fixed up a little kitchen in a closet, he had hung a salami and two ropes of garlic from the ceiling and had pinned an aerial view of Turin on the wall, along with a photo of the city's football team all covered with autographs. As Penates go, these weren't much, but I didn't have even them, and I felt more at home in his room than in mine. When the tea was ready he served it to me politely, but without a tray, and he advised—or rather prescribed—the addition of some vodka, at least half-and-half, "then you sleep better." But in that remote dormitory, we slept well in any case; at night you could enjoy a total, primordial silence, broken only by the breath of the wind and the sob of an unidentified nocturnal bird.

"Well then. The friend I was saddest of all to leave, when I tell you who it was, you'll be knocked out of your seat. Because first of all he got me into real trouble, and second because he wasn't even a Christian. That's the truth. He was a monkey."

I wasn't knocked out of my seat: thanks to a deeply rooted habit of self-control, by which second reactions precede the first, but also because Faussone's prologue had blunted the edge of the surprise. I must have said already that he isn't a great raconteur, and he is more successful in other areas. For that matter, there was nothing so amazing: who doesn't know that the best friends of animals, the best at understanding them and being understood, are the lonely?

"For once, it wasn't a crane. I would still have a lot of stories about rigging cranes, but a guy can become boring in the end. That time it was a derrick. Do you know what a derrick is?"

I had only a notion from books; I knew they are steel towers, and they are used to drill oil wells, or perhaps to extract the oil itself. On the other hand, if he cared to know, I could give him some information about the origin of the name. Mr. Derrick, a man of parts, conscientious and devout, lived in London in the seventeenth century and for many years was hangman for their Britannic Majesties; he was so conscientious and so enamored of his profession that he constantly pondered ways to perfect his instruments. Toward the end of his career he developed a new model gallows, a tall, slender tower, thanks to which the man hanged, "high and close," could be seen from a distance. This was called the *Derrick gallows*, and then, more familiarly, *derrick*. Later, the term came to cover analogous structures, all in trestle form, destined to humbler uses. In this way Mr. Derrick achieved that special and very rare form of immortality that consists in the loss of the capital letter at the beginning of one's surname: an honor shared by no more than a dozen illustrious men of all time. But Faussone should please go on with his story.

Faussone accepted, without batting an eye, my frivolous interjection. But he had assumed a remote look, perhaps made uneasy by the fact that I had used the subjunctive, in the style of an oral exam in school.

Then he continued: "That may very well be. But I always thought they hanged people any old way. In any case, this derrick was nothing special, maybe twenty meters, a drilling derrick, the kind that if they don't find anything they dismantle it and take it somewhere else. As a rule in my stories it's either too hot or too cold; well, this time, it was in a clearing in the midst of a forest, and it wasn't hot or cold, but instead it rained all the time. It was a warm rain, and you couldn't even say it was unpleasant, because there are no places to take showers in those parts. You just take off your clothes, down to your shorts the way the locals do, and if it rains, you let it rain.

"As far as the rigging went, it was laughable: there wouldn't even have been any need for a full-fledged rigger; any workman who could stand heights would've done. I had three workmen under me, but what a trio! My God! Maybe they were undernourished, sure, but all they were good for was loafing from morning to night. When you spoke to them, they didn't even answer; they seemed asleep. The fact is that I had to think of more or less everything: the generator, the hookups; I even had to do some cooking for myself in the hut at night. But the thing that concerned me most of all was what they call the boring machine, the moving element; I would never have believed it was so complicated: you know, the thing with all those belts and the worm screw, to bring down the drill bit. Rigging all that is a job that, strictly speaking, isn't in my line. It looks like nothing much, but inside there is the whole gadget for the feeding, which is electronic and self-regulating, and the controls for the pumps for the slurry; and from below you screw on the steel pipes that go down into the well one after the other. What I'm saying is it was a whole scene like you normally see . . . yes, in the movies, those pictures about Texas. I don't mind saying that's quite a job, too. I didn't realize, but you go down maybe five kilometers, and that doesn't necessarily mean there's any oil there, either."

After the tea and vodka, as Faussone's story showed no signs of getting off the ground, I made a cautious reference to a fermented cheese and some little Hungarian sausages I had in my room. He didn't stand on ceremony (he never does; he says that's not his style), and so the tea party began to develop into a snack or little supper, as the orange light of the sunset was shifting to the luminous violet of a northern night. Against the western sky a long rise of land stood out sharply, and above it, low and parallel, ran a thin, dark cloud, as if a painter had regretted a brush stroke and had repeated it a little higher. It was a strange cloud: we argued about it, then Faussone convinced me: it was dust raised by a distant herd in the windless air.

"I couldn't tell you why the jobs we get are always in crazy places: either sweltering or freezing, or parched, or it rains all the time, like the place I'm telling you about. Maybe we're just spoiled, coming from a civilized country, and if we land in some place a bit different, it seems right away like the end of the world. And, instead, all around there are people who get along fine in their country and wouldn't trade with us. It's all habit.

"Well then, in this country I'm telling you about, the people don't make friends easily. Mind you, I don't have anything against wogs, and in plenty of other places I've found some who are more on the ball than us, but down there it was another bunch altogether. They're slackers and liars. Very few speak English; I don't understand their language; no wine, they don't even know what it is; they're tight with their women, and I swear they're wrong, because the women are dumpy, with short legs and tits down to here. The stuff they eat would turn your stomach, and I won't go into detail because we're having supper. In other words, when I tell you the only friend I made down there was an ape, you can believe me: I didn't have any other choice. Even the ape wasn't all that good-looking: he was the kind that have like a fur coat around their head and a dog face.

"He was curious. He used to come and watch me work, and first thing he did, he showed me something. I told you, it rained all the time: well, he sat down to take the rain in a special way, with his knees raised, his head on his knees, and his hands clasped over his head. I noticed how in that position he had his hair all slicked downward, so he hardly got wet at all: the water ran off his elbows and his behind, and his belly and face stayed dry. I tried it myself, taking a bit of a rest between bolts; and I must say that if you don't have an umbrella that's the best solution."

I thought he was joking, and I promised him that if I ever found myself naked under a tropical rain, I would assume the monkey's position, but I immediately caught a look of irritation. Faussone never jokes; if he does, his jokes are as ponderous as a tortoise. And he doesn't like jokes from others.

"He was bored. At that season the females stay all together in a pack, with a tough old male who leads them and makes love with them all, and if he sees any young males lurking around, they're in trouble; he jumps on them and scratches them. I sympathized with my monkey's situation because it was sort of like mine, though I was without females for other reasons. You understand how it is, alone like that, the two of us, with the same melancholy; we quickly made friends . . ."

A thought crossed my mind: again we were alone, the two of us, and with a melancholy upon us. I had replaced the ape, and I felt a rapt wave of affection for that now-distant sharer of my fate, but I didn't interrupt Faussone.

". . . only he didn't have a derrick to rig. The first day he just hung around there and watched. He would yawn, scratch his head and belly, like this, with his fingers all limp, and he would show me his teeth: it's not like with dogs; when they show their teeth, it's a sign they want to make friends, but it took me a few days to understand him. The second day he circled around the case of bolts, and when I didn't shoo him away, he would pick up one every now and then and test it with his teeth, to see if it was good to eat. The third day he had already learned that each bolt goes with its nut, and he hardly made a mistake afterward: the half-inch with the half-inch, the three-eighths with the three-eighths, and so on. But he couldn't figure out that all the threads are right-handed. He never did understand that, not even later; he would try it any old way, and when it worked, and the nut would turn, then he would jump up and down, clap his hands on the ground, make some noises; and he seemed happy. You know something: it's really a shame that us riggers don't have four hands like apes do, and maybe even a tail. I was dying of envy. When he felt a bit more confident, he would come up the truss like a bolt of lightning, cling to the beams with his feet, head down, and in that position he would screw the nuts and bolts, and make faces at me.

"I tell you, I could've spent the whole day watching him, but I had a deadline, and that was that. I managed to get on with the job, between one downpour and the next, with what little work I could get out of my three good-for-nothing helpers. The ape could really have helped me, but he was like a kid: he thought it was all a game, a toy. After a few days I would signal to him to bring me up the pieces I needed, and he would scramble down and then up, but he would always bring me only the top ones, which were painted red, because of planes. They were the lightest, too: you could tell he had sense. He wanted to play, but he didn't want to strain himself.

But I tell you, those other three goons didn't do much more than he did, and at least he wasn't afraid of falling.

"A bit today, a bit tomorrow, I finally managed to set up the pulley rig, and when I tried out the two engines, at first he was kind of scared by the noise and all those wheels turning on their own. By this time I had given him a name: I would call him and he would come. Maybe because every day I gave him a banana, but anyway he came. Then I rigged the control cabin, and he was there watching like he was spellbound. When all those little red and green lights came on, he looked at me like he wanted to ask me all the reasons, and if I didn't pay any attention to him, he would whimper like a little boy. Well, at that point, no use denying it, it was all my fault what happened. I saw how all those buttons fascinated him too much. I mean, I was such a fool that the last night it never occurred to me that I had better unscrew the fuses."

A disaster was coming near. I almost asked Faussone how he could have committed such a serious oversight, but I restrained myself, to keep from spoiling his story. In fact, just as there is an art of story-telling, strictly codified through a thousand trials and errors, so there is also an art of listening, equally ancient and noble, but as far as I know, it has never been given any norm. And yet every narrator is aware from experience that to every narration the listener makes a decisive contribution: a distracted or hostile audience can unnerve any teacher or lecturer; a friendly public sustains. But the individual listener also shares responsibility for that work of art that every narration is: you realize this when you tell something over the telephone, and you freeze, because you miss the visible reactions of the listener, who in this case can only express his interest through an occasional monosyllable or grunt. This is also the chief reason why writers, those who must narrate to a disembodied public, are few.

". . . No, he didn't manage to smash it up completely, but he came close. While I was there messing with the contacts, because, you know, I'm not an electrician, still a rigger has to manage more or less in any situation; and especially afterward, while I was testing the controls, he didn't miss a move. And the next day was Sunday, and the job was over, and I needed a day of rest. Well, to make a long story short, Monday came, and when I went back to the site, the derrick looked like somebody had given it a slap. It was still standing, but all crooked, with the hook caught in the base, like the anchor of a ship. And there he was, sitting, waiting for me. He had heard me coming on my motorcycle. He was all proud; God knows what he thought he had done. I was sure I had left the boring machine up, but he must've lowered it: you only had to press a button, and on Saturday he'd seen me do it lots of times. And you could bet he'd been swinging on it, even though he weighed maybe half a ton. And while he was swinging, he must have sent the hook to snap onto a girder, because it was one of those safety hooks, with a spring catch, that when they close, they won't come open again. You see the tricks some security gadgets can play on you at times. In the end, maybe he had realized he was causing trouble and had pressed the lift button, or maybe it was only chance. The whole derrick had gone taut, and when I think about it, even now, my blood runs cold; three or four beams had given, the whole tower tilted, and it was a good thing the safety switch had worked; otherwise it would have been goodbye to your London hangman."

"But the damage wasn't serious, then?" As soon as I had uttered the question, from its anxious tone I realized I was siding with him, with the adventurous ape, who probably had wanted to emulate the wonders he had seen his silent human friend perform.

"That depends on how you look at it. Four days' work for the repairs and a stiff fine. But while I was there, working to straighten everything up, he changed expression. He was all in the dumps, his head pulled down between his shoulders, and he kept looking away. If I went toward him, he would run off. Maybe he was afraid I'd claw him, like the old male, the lord of the females. . . . Well, what are you waiting for now? The derrick story is over. I set it straight again, I had them run all the tests, I packed my suitcase, and I left. Even though the ape had caused all that trouble, I'd have liked to take him

home with me, but I thought that back here he would probably get sick. They wouldn't let me keep him in the pensione,
and he would have been some present for my aunts. And, for
that matter, I'm damned if he showed his face again."

THE BOLD GIRL

HELL, NO. Wherever they send me, off I go. In Italy, too, of course. But they hardly ever send me anyplace in Italy, because I'm too good at my job. Don't get me wrong: but the fact is I can handle almost any situation, so they prefer to send me abroad; and in Italy they send the young ones, or the old ones, guys who're afraid of a heart attack, and the lazy ones. For that matter, I like it better this way: seeing the world, you always learn something new, and I keep a safe distance from my boss."

It was Sunday, the air was cool, with a tang of resin, the sun seemed never to set, and the two of us were taking a walk through the forest with the idea of reaching the river before dark. When the rustle of the wind among the dead leaves stopped you could hear the river's deep, calm voice that seemed to come from all the points of the horizon. You could also hear at intervals, sometimes close, sometimes far off, a faint but frenzied hammering, as if someone were trying to drive nails into tree trunks with tiny pneumatic hammers: Faussone explained that they were green woodpeckers, and we have them back home, too, but it's forbidden to shoot them. I asked him if that boss of his was really so unbearable that he had to travel thousands of kilometers so as not to see him, and Faussone said no, actually he was all right, a term that, in Faussone's language, has a very broad meaning, signifying cumulatively a man who was meek, polite, expert, intelligent, and brave.

". . . but he's one of those guys who want to teach cats how to scratch, if you follow me. . . . He's oppressive, I mean; he won't give you any freedom. And on the job if you don't feel free, that's the end; there's no satisfaction, and you might as well transfer to Fiat: at least when you come home then you can put on your slippers and go to bed with the wife. It's a temptation, you know. It's a risk, especially when they pack you off to certain countries. No, not this one; here it's a bed of roses. There's the temptation, as I was saying, to give it up, get married, and end this gypsy life. Yes, it's a temptation, all right," he repeated, pensively.

Clearly the theoretical statement was to be followed by the practical example. And, sure enough, a moment later he resumed: "Like I was saying, that time the boss sent me to a place in Italy, or rather, in southern Italy, it was because he knew there was trouble. If you want to hear the story of a screwy job—and I know some people do enjoy hearing about others' misfortunes—then listen to this one, because I've never had a job like it again, and I wouldn't wish it on any rigger. First of all, because of the client. An all right sort of guy, too. I'll tell you, he invited me to some great meals and even put me up in a canopied bed, because he insisted I should be a guest in his home. But he didn't understand the first thing about the job, and you know there's nothing worse than that. He was in the salami business and he had made some money, or maybe he got some grant from the government; I couldn't say. The fact is he got it into his head to produce metal furniture. Only dopes believe it's best to have a dumb client, because that way you can do what you like. Not at all: a dumb client, on the contrary, does nothing but make trouble for you. He'll have the wrong equipment, won't lay in any spare parts; the first thing goes wrong he loses his temper and wants to rescind the contract; and when things go well he wants to talk and he wastes your time. At least, that's how this guy was, and I felt like I was between the hammer and the anvil, because at the other end of the telex there was my boss, who was on my neck. He would send me a telex every two hours, to know the state of the work. I have to tell you that bosses, when they've passed a certain age, they each have their manias, at least one, and my boss had several. The first and the worst, like I told you, was to do everything himself, as if you could rig a crane sitting behind a desk or hanging on to the phone or the telex. Imagine! Rigging something is a job that a person has to work out on his own, with his own head and, even better, with his own hands. Because, you know, seeing a job from a chair is one thing, and from a tower forty meters high is something else. But he had other manias, too. Bearings, for example: He wanted only Swedish, and if he happened to discover that on a job somebody had used any other kind, he would turn purple and hit the ceiling, whereas generally speaking he was the calm type. And it was all nonsense, anyway, because on jobs like the one I'm telling you about, which was a conveyor belt, long but slow and light, you can be sure any bearings will do; in fact, you could even use the bronze bushings my godfather used to make, one at a time, with elbow grease, for Diatto and for Prinetti in Turin, in his shop in Via Gasometro. That's what he used to call it; now it's called Via Camerana.

"And because he was an engineer, this boss also had a mania about fatigue failure; he could see it everywhere, and I think he even dreamed about it at night. Since you're not in that line, maybe you don't even know what it is. Well, it's a freak, and in all my career I've never seen even one surefire case of fatigue failure, but when a piece snaps, bosses, designers, foremen always agree: they can't do anything about it, it's the rigger's fault, and by that time he's far away and can't defend himself; or else it's stray currents, or fatigue, and they wash their hands of it, or try to, anyway. But don't get me off the track. That boss's strangest mania was this: he was one of those men who lick their finger before turning the page of a book.

I remember how my teacher in elementary school, the very first day, taught us it was bad to do that because of germs. Obviously, his teacher had skipped that lesson because he licked his finger every time. Actually, I noticed he licked his finger every time he was about to open anything: the desk drawer, a window, the safe. Once I saw him licking his finger before raising the hood of his Lancia."

At this point I realized that I, not Faussone, was losing the thread of the story, what with the all right but inexperienced client and the all right but obsessed boss. I asked him to be more clear and concise, but in the meanwhile we had come to the river, and for a few moments we stood there without speaking. It was more like an inlet of the sea than a river: it flowed with a solemn rustle along our bank, which was a high dike of reddish, friable earth, while the other bank could barely be discerned. Against the edge little waves broke, clean and transparent.

"Hmph, maybe I got kind of sidetracked by the details, but I swear it was a crazy job. First of all, I don't like to say it, but the local workers were all dopes: maybe they were good at swinging a hoe, but I wouldn't swear to that, either, because to me they seemed more in the loafer category; they were reporting sick every minute. But the material was the worst: the bolts you could find there, first there wasn't much assortment, and second they would make a dog vomit. I've never seen such stuff, not even in this country, where when it comes to shoddy they don't mess around, and not even that time in Africa I told you about. And with the base pads, it was the same: it looked like they had taken the measurements with their fingers. Every day it was the identical routine: hammer, chisel, pick; break up everything and pour on the fast-setting cement. I would grab the telex, because the telephone also worked only when the spirit moved it, and fifteen minutes later, the little machine would start tapping out furiously, the way telexes do, always in a hurry even when they're writing balls, and on the sheet I would read: 'Despite our instructions you have apparently used material of suspect origin,' or some such crap that had nothing to do with the situation, and I would feel really up the creek. My elbows turned to milk, as we say back home, and believe me it's not just a figure of speech; you really do feel your elbows go all soft and your knees, too, and your hands hang down and sway like a cow's tits, and you feel like changing profession. It's happened to me various times, but that time was the worst of all, and I've seen a few things in my life. Has it ever happened to you?"

It certainly has. I explained to Faussone that, in peacetime at least, it's one of the basic experiences of life: in work and not only in work. No doubt in other languages this milky flood, which comes to weaken and block *Homo faber*, can be described in more poetic images; but I know none more vigorous. I pointed out to him that, to experience it, you don't necessarily have to have a tiresome boss.

"Yeah, but that guy, I'm telling you, would've tried the patience of a saint. Believe me, it's not that I enjoy running him down, because, like I told you, he wasn't really bad; he just caught me in my weak spot, my pleasure in my work. I'd have been happier if he'd slapped a fine on me, I don't know, even a suspension, instead of those little hints, those passing references, that later, when you think about it, you feel you've been skinned alive. I mean, it was like all the hitches on that job, and not only the one, had been my fault, because I hadn't wanted to use Swedish bearings, when I actually had used them: it wasn't my money, after all. But he wouldn't believe me, or else he pretended not to believe me. Well, after each phone call I felt like a criminal, when really I had put my whole heart and soul into that job. But I put my heart and soul into all my jobs, you know that, even the dumbest; or rather, the dumber they are, the more I give to them. For me, every job I undertake is like a first love."

In the gentle sunset light we started on our way back, along a path barely marked in the thick of the forest. Contrary to his habit, Faussone had interrupted his story and was walking silently at my side, his hands behind his back, his eyes fixed on the ground. Two or three times I saw him take a breath and open his mouth as if he were about to resume speaking, but he seemed unable to make up his mind. He spoke only when we were finally in sight of the dormitory.

"You want to know something? For once that boss was right. Almost right. It was true there were troubles on that job, you couldn't get the materials, and the Commendatore, the salami man, that is, instead of lending me a hand, would waste my time. It's also true there wasn't one workman who was worth a cent. But if the job proceeded badly, with all those delays, the fault was also partly mine. Or rather, a girl's."

Actually he used the dialect expression, 'na fija, and indeed, on his lips the proper Italian word, ragazza, would have sounded forced, unnatural; but it sounds equally forced to translate his term. In any case, this was surprising news: in all his other stories, Faussone had made a point of presenting himself as refractory, a man of scant sentimental interests, one who doesn't "run after girls," but one whom the girls, on the contrary, do run after, though he pays them little mind, takes this one or that; never very serious, keeping her as long as the job lasts, then telling her goodbye and leaving. I became alert, keen.

"You know they tell a lot of stories about the girls from down there, how they're short, fat, jealous, and good only for making babies. This girl I mentioned, she was as tall as I am, with almost-red brown hair, straight as a pole, and independent like very few I've ever seen. She drove a forklift. In fact, that was how we met. Next to the belt I was setting up there was a passage for the lifts: two could just barely get by. I see one lift coming down with a girl driving it, carrying a load of section irons, sticking out a bit; and coming up was another lift, empty, also with a girl driving. Obviously, they couldn't pass; one of the two would have to reverse as far as an open space, or else the girl coming down would have to unload and reload more carefully. Nothing doing. The two of them sit there and start cussing each other out good and proper. I caught on right away that there was a long-standing feud between them, and I was all ready to wait patiently until they finished, because I had to get by, too. I had one of those little carts you steer with a rudder, loaded with the famous bearings that God forbid should spill and my boss hear about it.

"Well, I wait five minutes, then ten. Nothing. The pair goes right on like they were at the fish market. They were fighting in their dialect, but you could understand almost everything. At a certain point, I stepped in and asked them please to let me by. The big girl, the one I'm telling you about, she turns and says to me, calm as you please: 'Hang on a minute. We haven't finished!'

"Then she turns to the other, and, cool as a cucumber, she says something to her that I wouldn't dare repeat, but I swear it made my hair stand on end. 'Now,' she says to me, 'you can go by,' and with this, she sets off in reverse, at top speed, scraping the columns and also the supports of my conveyor belt, making me feel like ice. When she got to the cross-passage at the end, she took the curve better than any Niki Lauda, still in reverse, and instead of looking behind her, she was looking at me.

"Christ! I was thinking to myself, this girl's a devil. But I had already figured out that she was staging the whole show for my benefit, and a little later I also realized that she was deliberately acting rude like that, because she had been watching me for several days, while I was putting the bubble on the brackets. . . ."

This expression sounded funny to me, and I asked him to explain. Irked, Faussone explained in a few chosen words that by bubble he meant a level, which contains, in fact, a liquid with an air bubble. When the bubble fits exactly into a marked space, then the level is perfectly horizontal, and so is the shelf or surface the level has been placed on.

"For example, we always say, 'Put a bubble on that support,' and the other guy understands. But let me go on: the story of this girl is more important. Anyway, she had understood me, that is, how I like people with minds of their own, people who know their job, and I had understood that, in her way, she was after me and was trying to strike up a conversation. Then we did start a conversation, and there was no hitch: I mean we went to bed together, everything regular, nothing special. But, yes, there was one thing I wanted to tell you: that the most beautiful moment, the one where you say, 'This is something I'll never forget, even when I'm an old man, as long as I live,' and you wish time would stop, like when an engine jams:

well, it wasn't when we went to bed, but before. It was at the mess hall of the Commendatore's factory; we sat down side by side, we finished eating, we were talking about this and that; in fact, I remember I was telling her about my boss and his way of opening doors, and I touched the bench on my right, and her hand was there and I touched it with mine, and she left her hand there and I could stroke it, like a cat. I tell you, everything that came afterward was pretty good, but it doesn't count as much."

"And now?"

"I swear, you really want to know everything," Faussone answered, as if I had been the one who asked him to tell the story of the forklift driver. "What can I tell you? It's a see-saw. Marry her? I can't do that: first because of my job, and second because . . . well, before a man marries, he has to think about it a lot, and taking a girl like that, fine girl, no two ways about it, but smart as a witch, well, I don't know if I'm making myself clear, but I can't seem to call it quits and not think about it anymore either. Every now and then I go to my boss and I get myself sent to that town, with the excuse that I have to check that thing out. Once she turned up in Turin, on vacation, with an old faded pair of bluejeans, cut off at the knees, and a boy in tow, one of those characters whose beard comes up to his eyes, and she introduced him to me like it was all normal, and I acted like it was normal, too. I felt a kind of heartburn, here, at the top of my stomach; still I didn't say a word, because that was the bargain. But you know something? You're quite a guy, making me tell these stories that, except for you, I've never told anybody."

TIRESIAS

As a RULE it doesn't work this way; as a rule he's the one who comes bursting in, with some adventure or misadventure to narrate, and he spills it all out in one breath, in that sloppy way of his that I've become used to by now, never letting himself be interrupted except by some brief request for clarification. So the tendency is more toward monologue than dialogue, and further, the monologue is encumbered by his repetitive tics, and by his language, which tends to be gray. Perhaps it's the gray of the fogs of our city, or perhaps it's the gray of steel beams and plates, the actual heroes of his stories.

That evening, however, things seemed to be proceeding differently. He had had a lot to drink, and the wine, which was a nasty, murky wine, had had some effect. It hadn't fuddled him, and for that matter (he says), a man in his line of work must never let himself be caught off guard; he must be always on the *qui vive* like the secret agents you see in the movies. It hadn't clouded his mind, but had somehow stripped him, had broken through his armor of reserve. I had never seen him so taciturn, but, strangely, his silence created more closeness than distance.

He drained another glass, without greed or appreciation, rather with the bitter stubbornness of someone swallowing a medicine. ". . . so these stories I tell you, you write them down afterward?"

I said yes, perhaps I did. I hadn't had my fill of writing; writing was my second profession, and, just at that time, I was thinking that it might be a good idea to make it my first profession, or my sole profession. Didn't he want me to write down his stories? On other occasions he had seemed pleased, actually proud.

"Yeah. Well, pay no attention. You know how it is: not all days are alike, and today's a bad day, the kind when nothing seems to go right. There are times when a man loses even his will to work." He was silent for a long moment.

Then he resumed: "That's right: there are days when everything goes wrong, and it's all very well to say a man isn't responsible, that the blueprint is a mess, that you're tired and, what's more, the devil's own wind is blowing. All that is true, but the lump you feel in your throat: nobody's going to get rid of that for you. Then you begin to ask yourself questions, maybe even questions that don't make sense, like for example, what are we in this world for? And if you think about it, you surely can't answer that we're in this world to rig towers. Right? In other words, when you break your neck for twelve days, putting everything you've got into the job, and you sweat and freeze and curse, and then you begin to have doubts, and they gnaw at you, and you check, and the job is crooked, and you can hardly believe it because you don't want to believe it, but then you check again and, sure enough, the dimensions are screwed up, then you want to know what happens. Then a man changes his way of thinking; and he begins to think that nothing's worth the effort, and he'd like to have another kind of job, and at the same time he thinks that all jobs are the same, and that the world is also crooked, even if we can go to the moon now, and it's always been crooked, and nobody's ever going to straighten it up, and least of all a rigger. Yeah, that's how you start thinking. . . . But, tell me something: does it happen to you people, too?"

How obstinate is the optical illusion that always makes our neighbor's troubles look less severe and his job more lovable! I answered that it was hard to make comparisons; but, in any case, having also done jobs similar to his, I had to grant him that to work sitting down, in a heated place and at ground level, is quite an advantage; but, aside from this, assuming I could speak in the name of actual writers, we have our bad days, too. In fact, we have them more often, because it's easier to see if a piece of metal structure is "right on the bubble" than a written page; so you can write a page with enthusiasm, or even a whole book, and then you realize it won't do, that it's a botch, silly, unoriginal, incomplete, excessive, futile; and then you turn sad, and you start getting ideas like the ones he had that evening, namely you think of changing jobs, air, skin, and maybe even becoming a rigger. But it can also happen that you write some things that really are botched and futile (and this happens often) but you don't realize it, which is far more possible, because paper is too tolerant a material. You can write any old absurdity on it, and it never complains: it doesn't act like the beams in mine tunnels that creak when they're overburdened and are about to cave in. In the job of writing the instruments, the alarm systems are rudimentary: there isn't even a trustworthy equivalent of the T square or the plumbline. But if a page is wrong the reader notices, and by then it is too late, and the situation is bad, also because that page is your work, only yours: you have no excuses or pretexts; you are totally responsible.

At this point I noticed that Faussone, despite the effects of the wine and his ill humor, had become alert. He had stopped drinking, and he was looking at me; his face, usually blank, steady, less expressive than the bottom of a pan, had a half-sly, half-malignant air.

"True, that's a fact. I'd never thought of that. Just think: for us guys, if they'd never invented control instruments, and we had to do the job just by guesswork . . . it'd be enough to drive you crazy!"

I told him that writers' nerves, in fact, tend to be a bit weak;

but it's hard to determine whether the nerves weaken because of the writing and the above-mentioned lack of sensitive instruments to evaluate the quality of the written matter, or whether the job of writing characteristically attracts people inclined to neurosis. There is, in any case, documentary evidence that numerous writers were neurasthenic, or became so (it's always hard to decide about "occupational diseases"), and others actually ended up in the asylum, or its equivalent, not only in this century, but also long before; and many, too, without contracting an occupational illness, live badly, are melancholy, drink, smoke, can't sleep, and die young.

Faussone was beginning to enjoy this game of comparing the two professions; to admit it wouldn't have been his way, which is all sobriety and reserve; but you could tell by the fact that he stopped drinking, and his silence was breaking down.

"The fact is," he replied, "that everybody talks a lot about labor, but the ones who talk loudest are the very ones who've never had the experience. If you ask me, the business of nerves snapping, nowadays, happens to pretty much everybody, writers or riggers or any other job. You know who it doesn't happen to? Doorkeepers and clock-watchers, the ones on the assembly line, because they're the ones who send the others to the loony bin. And while we're on the subject of nerves, you needn't think that when a man is up there at the top, by himself, and the wind is blowing, and the structure still hasn't been braced, and it's dancing like a boat on the waves, and you see people on the ground like ants, and you're hanging on with one hand and pulling your socket wrench with the other, and it would be nice to have a third hand to hold the blueprint and maybe even a hand number four to shift the hook of the safety belt: well, as I was saying, you needn't think it's all that good for the nerves. To tell you the truth, just offhand I can't think of a rigger who's ended up in the bin, but I know plenty, including friends of mine, who got sick and had to change their line of work."

I had to admit that, in fact, on the other side occupational illnesses are few, also because, generally speaking, working hours are flexible.

"You mean there aren't any," he said, sharply interrupting.

"A man can't get sick from writing. At worst, if he writes with a ballpoint, he can get a callus here. And when it comes to on-the-job accidents, we'd better just change the subject."

No question about it: he had scored a point, and I conceded it. But, equally a good sport, Faussone, with an unusual flight of the imagination, came out with the reflection that, basically, it was like deciding whether it was better to be born male or female: the only person who could say anything would have to be someone who had tried it both ways; and at this point, though I realized I was striking below the belt, I couldn't resist the temptation to tell him the story of Tiresias.

He seemed a bit uneasy when I told him that Jupiter and Juno, besides being husband and wife, were also brother and sister, a fact that, in school, they usually don't dwell on, but it must have had some significance for their menage. On the other hand, he showed real interest when I mentioned their famous argument about whether the pleasures of love and sex were more intense for the woman or the man. Curiously, Jupiter gave first place to women, and Juno to men.

Faussone interrupted again: "Right, it's like I was saying before: to decide, you'd need somebody who had experienced what it's like to be a man and what it's like to be a woman, but there's no such person, even if every now and then you read in the paper about the Navy captain who goes to Casablanca, has an operation, and then produces four kids. If you ask me, it's all balls invented by the papers."

"Probably. But at that time it seems there was an umpire available: Tiresias. He was a wise man of Thebes, in Greece, who had had a strange thing happen to him, many years before. He was a man, a man like me and like you, and one autumn evening—I imagine it was damp and cold, like tonight—he was crossing a forest when he came upon a tangle of snakes. He looked closer and realized there were only two of them, but they were very long and thick: a male and a female (obviously this Tiresias had sharp eyes, because I honestly don't know how you can tell a male python from a female, especially in the evening and when they're all tangled up together, so you can't see where one ends and the other begins), a male and a female, making love. Whether because he was shocked or envious, or simply because they were in his way, Tiresias took a stick and gave the pair a blow. Well, he felt a funny kind of stirring, and from being a man, he had turned into a woman."

Faussone, who is always excited by notions of humanistic origin, told me, with a snicker, how once, and not all that far from Greece, namely in Turkey, he had found in the woods a tangle of serpents: not two of them, but plenty, and not pythons, but grass snakes. They really seemed to be making love, in their way, all entwined; but he had nothing against that and had left them alone. "But now that I know the trick, next time it happens, I'd almost give it a try myself."

"Well anyway, it seems this Tiresias remained a woman for seven years, and as a woman he also had his share of experiences; then, when the seven years had gone by, he came upon the snakes again. And this time, knowing the trick, he deliberately gave them a blow: to become a man again, in other words. Obviously, all things considered, he believed manhood had more advantages. Anyhow, in that debate I was telling you about, he said Jupiter was right; I couldn't tell you why. Maybe because he had found himself better off as a woman, but only as far as sex went and not for the rest of it; otherwise, he would surely have stayed a woman, I mean he wouldn't have hit the snakes a second time. Or maybe he thought that if you contradict Jupiter you never know what may happen. But he got himself into serious trouble, because Juno took offense . . ."

"Eh, never come between husband and wife, as the saying goes . . ."

". . . she took offense and made him blind, and Jupiter could do nothing about it, because at that time there was apparently this rule: when a god inflicted some disaster on a mortal, none of the other gods, not even Jupiter, could cancel it. For want of anything better, Jupiter gave him the gift of foreseeing the future. But, as you can tell from this story, it was too late."

Faussone was toying with the bottle and had a vaguely irritated look. "That's not a bad story. You learn something new every day. But I don't exactly understand what's the point of it. Are you telling me that Tiresias is you?"

I wasn't expecting a direct assault. I explained to Faussone that one of the writer's great privileges is the possibility of remaining imprecise and vague, saying and not saying, inventing freely, beyond any rule of caution. After all, on the towers we construct they don't run any high-tension lines; if our structures fall, nobody gets killed, and they don't have to be wind-resistant. In other words, we're irresponsible, and no writer has ever been put on trial or sent to jail because his constructions came apart. But I also told him that, though I had only realized it in the course of telling him the story, I really did feel a bit like Tiresias, and not only because of my double experience. In distant times I, too, had got involved with gods quarreling among themselves; I, too, had encountered snakes in my path, and that encounter had changed my condition, giving me a strange power of speech. But since then, being a chemist in the world's eyes, and feeling, on the contrary, a writer's blood in my veins, I felt as if I had two souls in my body, and that's too many. But he wasn't to give this too much thought because the whole comparison was forced: working at the tolerance limit, or even beyond the limit, is the joy of our profession. Unlike riggers, when we manage to exceed tolerance, to make an impossible coupling, we are pleased, and they praise us.

Faussone, to whom on other evenings I had told all my stories, raised no objections and asked no more questions, and for that matter it was now too late to delve any deeper into the question. In any case, sustained by my condition as expert in the two pleasures, *doctus utriusque veneris*, though he was visibly sleepy, I tried to explain to him that all three of our professions, my two and his one, on their good days can give fullness: his, and the profession of chemist that resembles it, because they teach us to be whole, to think with our hands and with the entire body, to refuse to surrender to the negative days and to formulas that cannot be understood, because you then understand them as you go on. And finally our professions teach us to know matter and to confront it: the profession of writing, because it grants (rarely, but it does grant) some moments of creation, like when current suddenly runs through a circuit that is turned off, and a light comes on or a rotor moves.

We agreed then on the good things we have in common. On the advantage of being able to test yourself, not depending on others in the test, reflecting yourself in your work. On the pleasure of seeing your creature grow, beam after beam, bolt after bolt, solid, necessary, symmetrical, suited to its purpose; and when it's finished you look at it and you think that perhaps it will live longer than you, and perhaps it will be of use to someone you don't know, who doesn't know you. Maybe, as an old man, you'll be able to come back and look at it, and it will seem beautiful, and it doesn't really matter so much that it will seem beautiful only to you, and you can say to yourself "maybe another man wouldn't have brought it off."

OFFSHORE

Sure, I'm young still, but I've been in some tight spots, and it was always because of oil. They never find oil in great places, say at San Remo or on the Costa Brava. Not on your life. It's always in lousy, godforsaken places. The worst things that happened to me happened because they were looking for oil. And, to tell you the truth, my heart wasn't even in it, because everybody knows, after all, that the stuff is about to run out, so it's not worth the trouble. But you know how it is: when you've signed a contract, you go where they send you. And besides, to be honest, that time I was pretty glad to go, because it was Alaska.

"I haven't read all that many books, but I've read every single one Jack London wrote about Alaska, ever since I was a kid, and not just once, either. And I had my own idea of the place; but now that I've been there, excuse me for saying this to your face, I've begun to lose faith in the printed page. I mean, in Alaska I thought I'd find a place all ice and snow, and midnight sun, and dogs pulling sleds, and gold mines, and maybe even bears and wolves chasing you. That was the idea

I had of the place, I carried it around with me, almost without realizing, and when they called me into the office and said there was a job in Alaska, rigging a drill, I didn't think twice. I signed up, also, because there was extra hardship pay, and besides I'd been in the city three months and—I've told you this before—staying in the city isn't for me. I mean, I like it for three or four days, I have some fun, maybe take in a movie; I look up a certain girl, and we meet, and I like seeing her again and taking her to a grand supper at Il Cambio, and I feel great. I may even go and pay a visit to those two aunts of mine in Via Lagrange that I told you about. . . ."

He hadn't told me about these aunts, or at least he had never described them to me; I could have sworn to that. We had a brief argument on the subject, as each tried politely to hint that the other didn't pay attention.

Then Faussone dismissed the question curtly: "Skip it. They're a pair of aunts, very devout; they sit me down in the parlor and feed me chocolates. One is smart, the other not so smart. But I'll tell you about them another time.

"I was talking about Alaska, and how I don't like staying in the city. What I mean is, I can't be in neutral. You know, like those engines that have the carburetor a bit off, and if you don't keep gunning them, they die on you, and you risk burning the points. After a couple of days, I feel sick, I wake up in the night, with a sensation like I'm coming down with a cold, but I don't actually get one; I seem to forget to breathe, my head aches, my feet hurt, if I walk down the street everybody seems to be looking at me. In other words, I feel low. Once I even went to the company doctor, but he just made fun of me. And he was right; I knew what was wrong with me: I wanted to get moving. So, this time I'm telling you about, I signed the contract, I didn't even ask too many questions; I was satisfied to find out it was a new job, a joint venture with the Americans, and I would get my instructions on the site. So all I did was shut my suitcase, because I keep it always ready, and I caught the plane.

"There's nothing to tell about the trip. In the old days jet lag used to bother me, but now I'm used to it. I changed three times, slept during the flight, and got there fresh as a daisy. Everything was going right: the salesman was there waiting for me in a Chrysler this long, and I felt like the Shah of Persia. He also took me to a restaurant to eat shrimp, sort of like our scampi, only bigger: he said they're the specialty of the country. But nothing to drink. He explained that he belonged to a religion where they can't drink, and he hinted politely that it was better for me not to drink either, because of my soul. He was a nice guy, but that's how he was. Between shrimps he also explained the job to me, and it sounded like an ordinary sort of job, but you know how salesmen are: they're good at handling people, but when it comes to work, forget it. Once I even got into a fight with one, just because he didn't understand a damn thing and was making impossible promises to the client. And you know what he said to me? That a job like ours can be understood completely, or understood partly, or else not understood at all; but to understand it completely you have to be an engineer, and rather than understand it partly, it's more elegant not to understand it at all: then you always have an out. What a way to think, eh?"

Since I have some friends who are salesmen, I did my best to defend the profession, saying that it's a delicate assignment, and often if they know too much it's worse, because they lose sales, and so on.

But Faussone wouldn't listen to reason: "No, no, I never met one who understood a thing or even made an effort. Sure, some of them pretend to understand, but they're the worst of all. Don't mention salesmen to me, if you want us to stay friends. Believe me, all they're good for is handling clients, taking them to nightclubs and football games; and that isn't so bad for us, either, because sometimes they take us along, too. But when it comes to knowing about the job, nothing doing, they're all alike. I never saw one that knew a thing.

"Well then, my man there tells me that this job is to finish assembling a derrick, at a work site about forty kilometers away, then to load it onto a boat and take it out to sea, on a shoal not far off. So I figured that if it was going to be loaded onto a boat, it must be a fairly ordinary derrick, and I was almost mad because they'd brought me all the way up there from the other end of the world. But I kept my mouth shut; it wasn't his fault.

"It got late. He says good night, and tells me he'll come by the hotel and pick me up at eight in the morning to take me out to the site, and then he goes off. In the morning, everything was fine, except there was shrimp again for breakfast; but I've eaten worse, after all. Everything fine, I was saying: he shows up at eight, right on the dot, with his Chrysler, and we set off, and we're outside the city in a minute, because it's a small town. Not exactly *Burning Daylight!* I've never seen a sadder country in my life: it looked like Sestriere, or any other ski resort, out of season; I don't know if you've ever been there. The sky was low, dirty, like you could almost touch it, because when the road started to climb, you went into the fog. There was a chilly little breeze, damp, that got inside your clothes and put you in a bad humor, and the grass in the fields all around was black, short and hard, like drill bits. Not a soul in sight, just some crows as fat as turkeys: they watched us go by and danced on their feet, not flying off, like they were laughing at us. We passed a hill, and from the top of the hill Mr. Compton pointed out the camp, in the midst of the gray air on the shore of the sea. I was speechless. You know me, and you know I don't like big talk, but we were still ten kilometers away and the thing seemed already there: it looked like the skeleton of a whale, long and black, lying on the shore, already rusted, because up there iron rusts in a minute; and I was thinking how I had to set it up in the open sea, and I felt faint. It's easy enough to say: 'Go and set up a derrick.' You remember the other time? The story with the monkey, when you told me about the hangman in London and all. Well, say that one was twenty meters high, and it seemed pretty high to me; but this one, not even finished, lying there, was two hundred and fifty meters long, like from here to that green fence over there, like from Piazza San Carlo to Piazza Castello, to give you an idea. Work never scares me, but right then and there I said to myself, My hour has struck.

"As we drove down the hill, Mister explained to me that

there is an Alaska with snow and sleds, but a lot farther north. Here was also Alaska, but a kind of annex that stretched down along the coast of the Pacific, a kind of handle to the real Alaska. And, in fact, they call it the Panhandle. And as for snow, he told me not to worry: this was the season, and one of these days it would come, and if it didn't, all things considered, we'd be better off. He almost seemed to know what was about to happen. As for the derrick, he said it was fairly big, all right, but that was why they had sent for a smart guy from Italy. All modesty aside, he meant me. He really was nice, except for that business about the soul.

"While we were talking, we went down the curves of the hill and got to the camp. There was a whole team waiting for us: the designers; the engineer in charge of the job; a half-dozen other engineers, freshly hatched, all spik-Englis, and all with beards; and the crew of Alaskan riggers, though not one of them was from Alaska. One guy was a kind of huge, hefty pistolero, and they told me he was a Russian Orthodox, because there still are some around there, ever since the Russians pulled off that big deal and sold Alaska to the Americans. The second one was named Di Staso, so obviously he couldn't have been a native Alaskan. The third was a redskin, they told me, because they're good at climbing up scaffoldings and aren't afraid of anything. I don't remember the fourth guy so well: he was a normal type, the kind you come across everywhere, with a retarded look.

"The head engineer was on the ball, one of those men who don't talk much and never raise their voice; actually, to tell the truth, I had a little trouble understanding what he said, because he talked without opening his mouth; but, you know, in America they teach them that in school: that it's not polite to open your mouth. Anyway, he was on the ball; he showed me the scale model, he introduced me to the crew I told you about, and he told me I'd be in charge of the operation. We went to eat dinner in the mess hall, and I don't have to tell you it was shrimp again; then he gave me the booklet with my instructions and said he would allow me two days to study it. After that, I should come back to the camp because we had to start work. In the booklet he showed me how all the operations had to be done on a set day, some even at a set hour, because of the tide. That's right, the tide. You can't understand that, can you? I didn't understand, either, at first, what the tide had to do with it; but I understood later, and I'll tell you about it later, if that's all right with you."

It was all right with me: it's always best to go along with the person telling the story; otherwise he gets blocked and loses the thread. For that matter, Faussone seemed in great form, and as the story gradually unfolded, I could see him pull his head down between his shoulders, as he always does when he's telling something big.

"Then we left, Compton and me. But I have to tell you, too, that I had a funny feeling: as if that office, that mess hall, and especially those faces were all something I had seen before. Then I realized it was true: it was all stuff I'd seen in the movies, I couldn't tell you when or in what picture. Compton and me, like I said, left for the city: I was to go back to the hotel and study the booklet, but once the job was under way, the engineer had told me there would be a room reserved for me at the camp. When he said *guest room*, I didn't understand at first what the hell it was, but I didn't dare ask him, because, in theory, I knew how to speak English.

"Well then, we drove off in the beautiful Chrysler of my mister friend; and I kept quiet and pondered the operation. On the one hand, it was a terrific job, the kind you remember for a long while afterward and are glad you did it; on the other hand, that talk about the tide and the fact that the derrick had to travel by boat was a bit hard to digest. I have to tell you: I've never liked the sea much, the way it moves all the time, and the damp, the sea air. I just don't trust it, and it puts me in a bad mood. At a certain point I saw something funny: in the sky you could see the sun was kind of hazy, and there were two smaller suns, one on either side. I pointed it out to Compton, and I could see he was getting nervous. Sure enough, a little later, all of a sudden the sky turned dark, though it was still day, and in a minute it began to snow, and I had never seen snow like that before. It came down thick, first in little grains as hard as semolina, then like a fine dust that even got into the car's air intake, and finally in clumps the size of walnuts. We were still climbing, about a dozen kilometers from the camp, and we realized things were taking a bad turn. Compton didn't say anything; he just grunted a couple of times. I was looking at the windshield wiper, I could hear the engine straining more and more, and I thought to myself that if it stopped, we'd had it.

"Excuse me for asking, but have you ever done something really stupid?"

I answered that I had, more than once. But I couldn't understand the reason for the question.

Then Faussone went on: "Me, too, lots and lots of times, but nothing as dumb as what he did then. We were skidding like crazy, and the only thing was to stay in second gear, not put on the brakes, not step on the gas, and maybe give the windshield wiper a rest every now and then. Instead, he saw a straight stretch of road, grunted again, and stepped on the gas. The car swerved and did an about-face as smart as a soldier's, and stopped against the mountain, with the two left wheels in the ditch. The engine died, but the wiper kept on going back and forth like mad, digging two little windows on the windshield, framed in snow. It was a good make, obviously, or maybe in places like that they soup them up.

"Compton was wearing city shoes and I had on army boots with rubber soles, so I had to get out and see what could be done. I found the jack and tried to set it up; I was thinking of raising the left side and then putting some stones under the wheels, in the ditch, and then trying to start off for the camp, since the car had made a half-turn anyway and was in a position to go downhill, and there didn't seem to be any damage. But nothing doing: it had stopped about a foot from the rock face, so I could barely slip in sideways. When it came to crouching down and placing the jack firmly, that was out of the question. Meanwhile, several inches of snow had fallen, and it was getting worse, and by now it was almost dark.

"All we could do was resign ourselves, sit there calmly, and wait for daybreak. Then we'd find a way of getting out of the snow. We had plenty of gas, we could leave the motor running and the heater, and we could sleep. The important thing was not to lose your head, but Compton had lost his right away: he was laughing and crying, he said he felt like he was smothering, and while there was still a ray of light, I ought to hurry to the camp for help. At a certain point he even grabbed me by the neck, so then I gave him a couple of punches in the stomach to calm him down, and he calmed down. But I was actually afraid to spend the night there with him, and anyway you know how I hate being cramped or cooped up. So I asked him if he had a flashlight, and he did. He gave it to me, and I jumped out.

"I must say things looked bad. The wind had risen, the snow had become fine again and was being driven sideways; it got down the back of your neck, into your eyes; and I had trouble breathing. Maybe a foot and a half had fallen, but the wind had piled it up against the rock and the car was almost buried. The headlights were still burning, but they were under a layer of snow, too, and you could see the light from above it, a dull glow that seemed to come from Purgatory. I knocked on the window, I told Compton to turn them off, to stay there quietly, and I'd be back soon. I tried to impress the car's position firmly in my mind, and I started walking.

"At the beginning it wasn't too bad. I told myself that, after all, I only had to go about ten kilometers, less if I flung myself down the shortcuts between one curve and the next. And I also told myself: You wanted Alaska, you wanted snow, and now you've got it, you should be pleased. That ten kilometers was like forty, because at every step I sank in up to my knees. And though I was walking downhill, I began to sweat, my heart was pounding; and partly because of the blizzard, partly because of the effort, I was gasping, and I kept having to stop for breath. The flashlight was practically no use: all you could see was lots of horizontal white lines, and a sparkling powder that made your head swim: so I turned it off and went ahead in the dark. I was in a big hurry to get down to the flat, because I thought that once I reached the bottom of the hill, the camp couldn't be far away. Well, it was stupid of me to hurry, because when I did get down to the flat, I realized I didn't know which way to go. I didn't have any kind of compass: until then my only guide had been the slope, and when that ended, I had no idea what to do. I was overcome by fear, and fear's an ugly animal, and I don't think I've ever been more afraid than I was at that moment, not even other times when, if I think about it, the danger was much worse. But here it was the darkness, the wind, the fact that I was alone in a country at the end of the world; and I thought that if I fell and lost consciousness the snow would bury me, and nobody would find me until April, when it thawed. And I was also thinking about my father, and I hardly ever think about him.

"My father, you know, was born in 1912, a bad generation. He was in all the wars you can think of—Africa, then France, Albania, and finally Russia—and he came home with a frostbitten foot and some weird ideas, and afterward he was a prisoner in Germany; but I'll tell you about that another time. I might add that it was then, while he was getting over his bad foot, that he put me into production. He always used to say that, joking about it. Anyway, this time I felt kind of like my father when they sent him off to get lost in the snow, though what he was was a good coppersmith; and he used to tell me how he just felt like sitting down in the snow and waiting to die, but instead he pulled himself together and walked for twenty-four days until he was out of enemy territory. And so I pulled myself together, too.

"I pulled myself together and I said to myself that the only thing was to use my head. I figured this way: if the wind had blown the snow against the car, that meant it was coming from the north, from the direction of the camp. In other words, I just had to hope the wind wouldn't shift direction and to keep walking into the wind. Maybe I wouldn't find the camp right off, but I'd get close to it, at least, and I'd avoid the danger of going in circles like a damn cockroach when you turn on the light. So I kept walking against the wind, and every now and then I'd turn on the flash to see my prints behind me, but the snow blotted them out in a minute. Besides the snow still falling from the sky I could see other snow, lifted by the wind, which scuttled along the ground into the darkness and whistled like a hundred snakes hissing. Every now and then I'd look at my watch, too, and it was funny: I felt I'd been walking for a month, but the watch didn't seem to move, like time had stopped. All the better for Compton, I thought; this way, we won't find him stiff as a cod. But I was willing to bet it seemed long to him as well.

"Anyway, I was lucky. After walking for two hours, I didn't find the camp, but I realized I was crossing the railroad, the service line. The tracks were invisible, of course, but you could see those fences they use up there to keep the snow from collecting on the tracks. They're no use at all for that, but they were of use to me, because they still stuck out a bit. And so, following the line of the fence, against the wind, I got to the camp. The rest went smoothly. They had a half-track they used in an emergency, as they call it, and I tell you, English really is a funny language, because with that snow nothing was emerging at all. It was a six-ton monster, with tracks a yard wide, and so it didn't sink into the snow and could climb a forty-degree slope like it was a joke. The driver turned on the headlights, we were back up there in a minute, found the place, and with our shovels we dug out Compton, who was half asleep. Maybe he had already begun to ice up, but we gave him a good shake, and a slug of liquor, which was against his principles, but he didn't notice. We massaged him, and then he was all right. He didn't talk much, but he was never one for talking. We left the car where it was.

"At the camp they fixed me up with a cot, and the first thing I did was ask for another copy of the instruction booklet, because the one they'd given me was going to spend the winter in the Chrysler. I was dead tired, and I fell asleep right away; but all that night I did nothing but dream of the snowstorm, and a man walking through it, in the night and the wind, and in the dream it wasn't clear if that man was me or my father. However, in the morning, the minute I woke up, I remembered that other emergency ahead of me, in a couple of days, the business of getting that outsize thing onto a boat and carrying it between one island and the next for about eighty miles, before setting it on the bed of the sea. Look, if you don't mind my saying so, from your expression I'd guess you don't understand all this."

I reassured Faussone: I promised him I was following his story with interest (which was true) and with complete comprehension. This was a bit less true, because certain feats you have to perform in order to understand them. Or, at least, you have to see them. He sensed this and, without hiding his impatience, he dug out a ballpoint, took a paper napkin, and said he would show me. He's good at drawing: he roughed out the form of his derrick, in scale: a trapezoid, 250 meters high, with the longer base of 105 meters and the shorter of 80, and on top of this another network of trusses, cranes, and turrets. Beside it he sketched the Mole Antonelliana in Turin, and the monument looked fairly sad; then he sketched St. Peter's, which just about came to the halfway mark.

"There," he said, pointing to the shorter base, "the sea comes up to here, after the thing's on its feet; but they assembled it on its side, already mounted on three sledges, and the three sledges are on three ramps of reinforced concrete and steel. All this was already done when I got there. Now I'll draw that for you, too. But the smart thing, the real trick was this: you can see it in the drawing: the six legs of the derrick platform aren't all the same. I've made the three on this side—you see?—thicker. And they were thick: three lengths of cylinder with a diameter of eight meters, and they were a hundred thirty meters long, the height of St. Peter's, here next to it. By the way, you know I don't hold with priests, but obviously when I went to Rome, I visited St. Peter's, and I must say they did a really great job, especially when you think of the equipment they had in those days. Well, in St. Peter's I didn't feel like praying, not even for a minute; but here, when that contraption turned slowly in the water and then stood up erect, on its own, and we all climbed on to it to smash the bottle, well, yes, I did feel like it a little. Too bad I didn't know what prayer to say; none seemed to fit. But I'm getting ahead of myself.

"Like I was saying, three of the legs are thicker. That's because they're not just legs; they're also floats, all carefully figured out. But to get back to my story. Well, I settled down at the camp, and I spent two days peacefully reading the booklet, discussing details with the engineer, and drying out my clothes. The third day we began work.

"The first job was to set up the hydraulic jacks; they're like jacks for cars, only bigger. It wasn't a hard job, and it was the ideal way to find out how good the crew was that I told you about: the Russian Orthodox, Di Staso, the redskin, and the normal guy. Needless to say, besides not understanding very well what I told them, they didn't understand each other too well, either. But, after all, they were riggers, and we always find a way of explaining ourselves, even if we only use sign language. We catch on fast, and if one guy is smarter, you can be sure the other guy listens to him, even if he doesn't have any chevrons. It's the same the world over, and every time I remember my father, rest his soul, I think that if armies worked the same way, then certain things wouldn't happen, such as taking a coppersmith from the Canavese region and packing him off to Russia with cardboard shoes to shoot at Russian coppersmiths. And if governments worked the same way, then there wouldn't be any need of armies in the first place because there wouldn't be any need for wars, and the people with common sense would work everything out."

The way people think when they venture to spout opinions outside their own field! I tried cautiously to make him aware of the subversive, indeed revolutionary force lurking behind these words of his. Assign responsibility according to skill? Was he joking? That system might just be acceptable for riggers, but for other, more subtle and complex activities? I had no difficulty getting him back on the track.

"Mind you, I don't like giving orders or taking orders. I like to work on my own, that way I sort of put my signature on the finished job. But, as you can imagine, this job wasn't something for one man. So we got busy: after that blizzard I told you about the weather was pretty good again and we got on fairly well, but now and then the fog would come down.

It took me a little time to figure out the kind of guy each of them was, because we're not all alike, particularly foreigners.

"The Orthodox was strong as an ox. His beard grew up to his eyes, and his hair came down to here, but he was a neat worker, and you could tell right away he was a pro. Only you couldn't interrupt him; if you did, he lost his bearings, went to pieces, and had to start all over again from the beginning. Di Staso, it turned out, was the son of a man from Bari and a German woman, and he actually did look like a kind of mongrel. When he talked, it was harder to understand him than a genuine American from America, but luckily he didn't talk much. He was the kind who always says yes and then does things his own way: I mean, you had to watch out, and the trouble with him was that he couldn't stand the cold, so he had to stop all the time, and he would jump up and down, maybe even at the top of the tower, and it gave me goose pimples when he put his hands under his armpits. The redskin was a character; the engineer told me he came from a tribe of hunters, and instead of staying on the reservation and playacting for tourists, they agreed unanimously to move to the big cities and work washing the windows of skyscrapers. This guy was twenty-two, but his father and his grandfather had already been in that business. Not that it's the same thing. To be a rigger you also need brains. But he had brains. Still, he had some odd habits: he never looked you in the eyes, never moved his face, and seemed very stiff. But he was quick as a cat on the job. He didn't talk much, either. He was about as charming as a bellyache, and if you criticized him, he answered back, and even called you names, but luckily in his tribe's dialect, so you could pretend not to understand, and there were never any fights. Now I should tell you about the normal guy, but I still haven't figured him out. He really was a bit dumb; it took him a while to catch on to things, but he was willing and paid attention, because he knew he wasn't all that smart, and he did his best not to make mistakes. And, actually, he didn't make many; I really couldn't understand how he made so few. I felt sorry for him, because the others laughed at him, and he was pathetic, like a kid, even if he was forty and not much to look at. I tell you, the good thing about our work is that there's room for guys like him, and on the job they learn the things they never learned in school: only you have to be patient with them.

"Like I was saying, it wasn't much of a job to set up the jacks, to make the platform slide toward the sea. It didn't take a lot of effort or a lot of know-how; you just had to fix them properly level. We did it in a day, and then we began to push. But you mustn't think we just stood there and pushed by guess-work: there was a control booth, nice and heated, and there was even a Coke machine, closed-circuit television, and a phone link with the men working the jacks. All you had to do was press a button and you could see on the TV screen whether everything was aligned. Oh, I almost forgot: between the jacks and the sledges there were also piezometric cells, with their dials in the booth, so you could see the stress at any moment. And while I was sitting there in the booth, in a chair, in the midst of all those gadgets, I was thinking of my father and his sheets of metal, a bang here and another bang there, judging always just with his eye, hammering out any flaws, from morning till night in the little blackened shop with a sawdust stove; and I got a kind of lump here in my throat.

"But I couldn't stay long inside there; at a certain point I ran out into the cold, to see the platform moving. You couldn't hear a sound, just the wind, the hum of the oil pumps in the control station, and the sea sloshing against the docks, three hundred meters away; but you couldn't see it because of the fog. And in the midst of the fog, lost in more fog, the platform could be seen coming forward, big as a mountain and slow as a snail. I had regulated the controls according to what the booklet said, and the platform was moving half a meter per minute. You had to get close to see it move, but then it was quite a sight, and I thought of the times when an army would come down and nobody could stop it, or when the lava came out of the volcano and buried Pompeii, because with that bold girl, the one I told you about, I went to Pompeii one Sunday.

"Excuse me, but from the way you're looking at me, I'm still not sure you really understand what the job was. Well, there was this structure lying on its side on three sledges, and the sledges were on three tracks that sloped down to the sea, and eighteen jacks were gently pushing. The platform was built to float, but to make it easier to handle, it was supposed to be slipped onto two pontoons, steel barges, I mean, which had been filled with water, before I even got there, and set on the bottom of the basin, in the right position. Once the platform was in position above them, we would pump out the water and bring them up to the surface, so they would take the weight of the platform, holding it above water; and then we would tow the pontoons and the platform out to the shoal, sink the pontoons again, and stand the platform erect, on its legs.

"Everything went smoothly. The platform arrived at the basin without a hitch, and it was time to bring up the pontoons. No, sir. The wind had been blowing for a while, it had cleared away the fog, but it had begun to stir up the sea. Not that I have much experience of the sea, and this was the first job I'd ever had involving the sea, or rather involving *me* in it. But I saw the engineer sniffing the air like a hound, wrinkling his nose and grunting, as if to say things were taking a bad turn. In fact, on the day we were to set up the derrick, there were already some big waves. This was also covered in the booklet: no setting up if the waves were more than two feet high. Two feet! These were a lot higher, and so we took time out.

"We were off work for three days, and nothing special happened. We spent the time drinking, sleeping, playing cards. I even taught my four mates to play briscola, because with the wind, and in that great landscape I told you about, you didn't feel like going out and having fun; nobody did. The redskin amazed me: with his usual rude manner, and without looking me in the eyes, he made me understand that he was inviting me to his house and that it wasn't far away. Being a kind of lout, he wouldn't stay in the guest quarters with the rest of us, but went to his own house, a little wooden shack, where he lived with his wife. The others snickered, and I couldn't figure out why. I went, because I like to see the way people live; and when I was inside his shack, I realized he was motioning me to go to bed with his wife. His wife, exactly like him, looked away and didn't utter a word, and I felt awkward because there weren't any curtains in there, no privacy; and besides I was scared. So I blurted out something in Italian, which he wouldn't understand, and I left. Outside, there were the others, waiting. Then I realized why they had laughed, and they explained that in his tribe this was the custom, to offer your wife to your superiors. But they said I was right not to accept, because these people washed only with seal grease, and not that often.

"When the sea calmed down, we began to pump air into the pontoons. It was an ordinary little low-head pump, no bigger than that bench there, and it spun smoothly. It seemed almost impossible that it could do the whole job of raising thirteen thousand tons on its own. Imagine how many cranes that would take. But in two days, the pontoons calmly came up, we fastened them tight under their supports, and on the evening of the second day the platform was floating there, and it seemed eager to set out, but that was just an effect of the wind. I confess I felt a little jealous of the engineers who had worked it all out: that trick of making air, water, and time do the work. It would never have occurred to me, but I told you I'm not very familiar with water. In fact, I can't even swim, and one of these days I'll tell you why.

"I can't swim, but it didn't make any difference, because in that sea nobody would have done any swimming. It was the color of lead, and so cold that I don't understand how those famous shrimp lived, the ones they kept giving us in the mess, sometimes boiled, sometimes grilled. But I was told that this sea was full of fish. We all slipped on our life jackets, because these details were also in the booklet; we climbed onto the tugs, and off we went, dragging after us the platform, lying on the two pontoons like when you lead a cow to the market by the halter. For me this was the first time at sea, and I wasn't at ease, but I tried not to let it show, and I thought that once we got started on the job of setting up the structure, I would have other things on my mind and the uneasiness would pass.

The Orthodox was scared, too, but the other three weren't feeling any effects, except Di Staso, who was a bit seasick.

"I said we set out for the open sea, but that's just a manner of speaking: it wasn't open at all. Off that coast there was a whole mass of islands and sandbars, channels running into one another, some of them so narrow that the platform could just squeeze through lengthwise, and when I thought of what would happen if it got stuck, I broke out in a cold sweat. Luckily the pilot was smart and knew the way. I even went into the pilot's cabin to see how it worked; he was calm as could be, talking via radio with the pilot of the other tug, in that nasal voice all Americans have. At first I thought they were deciding the route to take, but instead they were discussing the baseball game."

I hadn't grasped very clearly the business of the pontoons: if the platform was built to float, couldn't it be launched directly at sea, without those complications? Faussone looked at me, dumbfounded; then he answered with that impatient patience of a man talking to an eager but somewhat backward child.

"Well, if it was Lake Avigliana, maybe you'd be right, but that was the Pacific, and I honestly don't know why those explorers gave it that name, seeing how it always has waves, even when it's calm; or at least, whenever I've seen it. And a gadget that long, even if it's made of steel, any little thing can bend it, because it wasn't meant to work in a horizontal position. Kind of like us, when you think about it. We need a flat bed in order to sleep. Well, the pontoons were necessary; otherwise there was a risk it would be bent out of shape by the waves.

"Like I was saying, we were on one of the tugs, and at first I was a bit scared, but then I got over it, because I was convinced there was no danger. They are great machines, those tugs: not comfortable, no, they're not built for cruises, but they're tough, well designed, without one rivet too many, and when you're on one, you immediately get an impression of extraordinary strength, and, in fact, they're used to tow ships much bigger than themselves, and there isn't a storm can stop them. After we'd been navigating for a while from one channel to the next, I got fed up standing there to look at the view, which was always the same, so I went below, into the engine room, to get an idea; and I must say I enjoyed myself, even if it's an exaggeration to call it a room, because there was barely enough space to turn around in. But those connecting rods and, even more, the shaft of the screw, I'll never forget. Or the galley, either, where all the frying pans are bolted to the wall, and to fix a meal the cook doesn't have to move, because everything's within reach. For that matter, when night came, we stopped and they passed out rations like in the army, but it wasn't bad, except for fruit they gave us shrimp with jam. Then we went to bed, in hammocks; it didn't even rock all that much, just enough to put you to sleep.

"In the morning we came out of that maze of channels, and I could breathe more easily. We had to go only about a dozen miles to get to the place, where there was already a buoy with a light and a radio, so it could be found even in the fog. And there was fog, all right. We got to the buoy about noon. There we moored the platform to some other buoys, so it wouldn't drift off on its own during the work; and we opened the vents of the pontoons, to sink them a little and then tow them away. I say 'we,' but actually I stayed on deck and the redskin went onto the pontoons, because of the whole bunch he was the one the sea bothered least. For that matter, it was done in a moment; we simply heard a big gust, like a sigh of relief, and the two pontoons were detached from the platform and the tugs towed them off.

"At this point, the chips were down: it was my turn to shine. Luckily the sea was almost calm. I put on the toughest face I could muster, and then with my four men I got into a little dinghy and we climbed up the ladders of the derrick. We had to run the checks, then remove the safety rods from the floating legs. You know how it is when you have to do something you don't like, but you force yourself, because when a thing has to be done you do it, especially if you have to make others do it too, even if one of the others is seasick or maybe has made himself sick deliberately, because I had my suspicions.

"Checking it all out was a long business, but it went well; the bending was no worse than anticipated. About the safety rods: I don't know if I made myself clear. Picture my platform like a sawed-off pyramid, floating on one of its faces, made of three aligned legs, the flotation pipes. Well, we had to give weight to the lower part of those legs, so they would sink, and the pyramid would turn over and stand erect. To weigh down the legs we had to let seawater in: they were divided into sections with airtight bulkheads, and each section had valves to let the air out and the water in at the proper moment. The valves were radio-controlled, but they had safety catches, and these had to be released first by hand, I mean by hitting them with a hammer.

"Well, it was right at this moment that I realized the structure was moving. Funny: the sea seemed still, there were no visible waves, but all the same the platform moved: up and down, up and down, very gently, like a cradle; and I began to feel my stomach was up here. I tried to fight it, and maybe I would have succeeded, if I hadn't happened to glimpse Di Staso, hanging on to a couple of bracings like Christ on the cross, emptying his guts into the Pacific Ocean from a height of eight meters. That did it. We finished the job all the same, but you know how it is: as a rule I want to do my work with a bit of class; and I'll spare you the details, but instead of cats we looked more like those animals—I can't remember their names— that you see in the zoo: they have an idiot face, they laugh all the time, their paws end in hooks, and they move slowly, clinging to branches, their heads hanging down. Well, except for the redskin, the four of us gave that impression, and I could actually see those bastards on the tug: instead of encouraging us, they were laughing and acting like monkeys, slapping their thighs. But from their point of view they must've been right: to see the big expert who had been brought specially from the other side of the world, with his socket wrench hanging from his belt, because for us it's what a sword was for knights in olden times, and there he is throwing up like a baby. It must've been a great sight.

"Luckily I had prepared that part of the job well, and I had made the four of them rehearse; so, except for the matter of elegance, we finished only fifteen minutes behind the schedule in the booklet, we got back onto the tug, and my seasickness went away at once.

"On the bridge there was the engineer, with binoculars and stopwatch, at the radio controls, and there the ceremony began. It was like watching TV with the audio off. He pressed the buttons one by one, like doorbells; only you couldn't hear anything, just us breathing, and we breathed like we were on tiptoe. And at a certain point, we saw the platform begin to tilt, like a ship when it's about to sink: even from the distance we could see the eddies the legs made as they sank into the water, and the waves came all the way to us and rocked the tug, but we couldn't hear any sounds. It tilted more and more; the top of the platform rose, until finally, with a lot of foam, it was on its legs. It sank just a little, then stopped abruptly, still like an island, but it was an island we had made; and I can't speak for the others—maybe they weren't thinking about anything—but I was thinking about the Almighty when he made the world, assuming he was the one who did, and when he separated the waters from the dry land, even if this didn't have much connection. Then we boarded the dinghy, the guys from the other tug joined us, and we all climbed onto the platform, we broke a bottle, and made some rumpus, because that's the custom.

"Now don't go telling this to anybody, but at that moment I felt like crying. Not because of the derrick, but because of my father. I mean, that metal monster anchored there in the midst of the water reminded me of a crazy monument my father made once with some friends of his, a piece at a time, on Sundays after their bowling, all of them old geezers, a bit loony, and a bit drunk. They had all been in the war, some in Russia, some in Africa, some God knows where, and they'd had a bellyful; so, since they were all more or less in the same line of work—one could weld, another could file, another could beat metal plate, et cetera—they decided to make a monument and give it to the town, but it was going to be a monument in reverse: iron instead of bronze, and instead of all the eagles and wreaths of glory and the charging soldier with his bayonet, they wanted to make a statue of the Unknown Baker, yes, the man who invented the loaf. And they were going to make it of iron, in heavy black plate, in fact, welded and bolted. They actually made it, and it was good and solid, all right, but as for looks, it didn't come out too well. So the mayor and the priest wouldn't accept it, and instead of standing in the center of the square, it's rusting in a cellar, among the bottles of good wine."

BEATING COPPER

THE PLACES WHERE my father was, during the retreat, must have been fairly near here. But it was a different season. He used to tell me about it: even the wine in the canteens froze, and the leather of the cartridge belts."

We had strolled into the woods, an autumnal forest splendid with unexpected colors: the green-gold of the larches, whose needles had just begun to fall; the dark purple of the beeches; and further, the warm brown of the maples and the oaks. The birch trunks, naked by now, made you want to pet them, like cats. Among the trees the underbrush was low, and the dead leaves were still few. The ground was firm and springy, as if packed, and it resounded strangely under our footsteps. Faussone explained to me that if you don't let the trees grow too thick, the wood cleans itself: the animals, large and small, take care of that, and he showed me the hare's tracks in the mud caked by the wind, and the red and yellow galls of the oaks and the dog roses, with a little worm asleep inside. I was somewhat amazed by this familiarity of his with plants and animals, but he reminded me that he hadn't been born a rigger. His happiest childhood memories involved snitching, little rural thefts, group forays in search of nests or mushrooms; self-taught zoology; theory and practice of traps; communion with the unassuming nature of the Canavese region, in the form of blueberries, strawberries, raspberries, blackberries, wild asparagus: all enlivened by the little thrill of the veto defied.

"Yes, because my father used to tell me," Faussone went on, "from the time I was a kid, he wanted me to get my schooling done with and come into the workshop with him. Be like him, in other words. By the time he was nine, he was already in France learning his job, because in those days that's what all of them did; in the valley there they were all coppersmiths, and he kept at the job until he died. That's what he used to say: he had to die with his hammer in his hand, and that's how he did die, poor man. But that isn't necessarily the worst death, either, because lots of men, when they have to give up working, they get an ulcer or take to drink or start talking to themselves, and I believe he would have been one of those men, but, like I said, he died first.

"He never did anything but beat copper, except when they took him prisoner and sent him to Germany. Copper plate: and from that copper—because in those days stainless steel wasn't the fashion yet—they made everything: pots, pans, water pipe, and even illegal stills to make bootleg grappa. In my town—because I was born there, too, during the war—all you could hear was hammering. Most of all, they made pots for cooking, big and little, coated with tin on the inside, because that was the traditional craft, the work of the *stagnino*, the man who makes pots and then coats them with tin, with *stagno;* and lots of people are still called Stagno or Magnino, and maybe they don't even realize why.

"As you probably know, when you hammer copper, it hardens. . . ."

I did know that; and as we talked, the fact emerged that, although I had never hammered metal plate, I did have an old acquaintance with copper, marked by love and by hatred, by silent, furious battles, enthusiasm and weariness, victory and defeat, resulting in more and more refined knowledge, as happens also with people if you live with them over a long time and finally can predict their words and movements. I knew, yes, the feminine, yielding quality of copper, the metal of mirrors, the metal of Venus; I knew its warm glow and its unhealthy taste, the soft blue-green of its oxide and the glassy blue of its salts. I knew well, through my hands, how copper hardened; and when I told Faussone, we felt a bit like relatives. When copper is maltreated—hammered, I mean, stretched, bent, compressed—it behaves as we do: its crystals grow and it becomes hard, tough, hostile. Faussone would have said *arvèrs*: adverse. I told him that I might be able to explain to him the mechanism of the phenomenon, but he said it didn't matter to him, and, besides, as he reminded me, it doesn't always work the same: just as we humans aren't all the same, and in the face of difficulty we behave in different ways, so some materials, like felt and leather, improve if you hammer them, and so does iron, which, if you hammer it, spits out the dross and becomes stronger. In fact, it turns into wrought iron, I told him, concluding that you have to be careful with similes, because they may be poetic, but they don't prove much, so you have to watch your step in drawing educational or edifying lessons from them. Should the educator take as his model the smith, who roughly pounds the iron and gives it shape and nobility, or the vintner, who achieves the same result with wine, separating himself from it and shutting it up in the darkness of a cellar? Is it better for the mother to imitate the pelican, who plucks out her feathers, stripping herself, to make the nest for her little ones soft, or the bear, who urges her cubs to climb to the top of the fir tree and then abandons them up there, going off without a backward glance? Is quenching a better didactic system than the tempering that follows it? Beware of analogies: for millennia they corrupted medicine, and it may be their fault that today's pedagogical systems are so numerous, and after three thousand years of argument we still don't actually know which is best.

In any case, Faussone reminded me that copper plate, once hardened (in other words, no longer workable by the hammer, no longer "malleable"), has to be annealed, that is: heated for a few minutes at a temperature of around 800 degrees centigrade, to regain its former suppleness. Consequently, the smith's job consists of alternately heating and hammering, hammering and heating. I knew these things more or less; but, on the other hand, I didn't have the same long familiarity with tin, to which I'm linked only by a fleeting youthful adventure—furthermore of an essentially chemical nature; so I listened with interest to the information he provided.

"Once the pot is made, the job still isn't finished, because, you know, for example, if you cook in a plain copper pot, afterward you fall sick, you and the family; and for that matter, the fact that my father died before he was fifty-seven may also be because he already had copper circulating in his blood. The moral of the story is that the pot has to be tin-plated on the inside, and you mustn't think that's so easy, even if you may know in theory how it's done. Theory is one thing and practice is another. Well, to make a long story short, first comes the vitriol, or if you're in a hurry, nitric acid—but just for a moment; otherwise it's goodbye pot—then you wash it with water, and then you remove the oxide with cooked acid."

This term was new to me. I asked for an explanation, but I never imagined that, in doing so, I was reopening an old wound, because it turned out that Faussone himself didn't know exactly what "acid cheuit" was, and the reason he didn't know was that he had refused to learn. There had been a bit of a quarrel with his father, in other words, because by then Faussone was eighteen and was fed up with living in the village and making pans. He wanted to go to Turin and get a job with Lancia, and he did, but it didn't last long. Well, the very cause of this disagreement had been cooked acid, and first his father got mad, then shut up, when he realized there was nothing to be done.

"Anyway, you make it with hydrochloric acid; you cook it with some zinc and some ammonium chloride, and I don't know what else. I can ask if you like. But you're not planning to coat any copper pans, are you? I should hope not. That isn't the whole business, in any case. While the cooked acid is at work, you have to have the tin ready. Virgin tin: this is where you tell whether the smith is honest or a crook. You need virgin tin, pure, in other words, like it comes from its home countries, and not soldering tin, which is a lead alloy. And I'm telling you this because there have been smiths who coated pots with soldering tin. There were some even in my town, and when the job is finished, you can't tell. But what happens to the purchaser then, when they cook for maybe twenty years with lead, and it slowly passes into all the food? I'll let you answer that one yourself.

"Well, I was saying you have to keep the tin ready, molten but not too hot; otherwise it forms like a red crust and you waste material. And, you know, these days it's easy, but then thermometers were stuff only rich people had, and you had to guess the heat with your eye, or by spitting. Sorry, but it's no good mincing words. You'd see if the spit sizzled or even jumped back. At this point you take the *cucce*, which are like thick strands of hemp, and I don't even know if they have a name in Italian, and you spread the tin on the copper like a person might smear the inside of a dish with butter. Is that clear? And the minute you're finished, you plunge it in cold water; otherwise, instead of being nice and shiny, the tin looks kind of clouded. You see, it was a job like any other job, with tricks of the trade, big and little, invented by God knows what Faussone at the beginning of time, and to tell you all the details it would take a whole book, and it's a book nobody will ever write, and actually that's a shame. In fact, now that all these years have gone by, I'm sorry about that argument I had with my father, the way I answered him back and shut him up, because he realized that this job, always done that same way, old as the world, was finally going to die with him, and when I told him that I didn't give a damn about cooked acid, he kept quiet, but he felt like he was already dying a little then. Because, you see, he liked his work, and I understand him now because I like mine."

This was the central subject, and I realized Faussone knew it. If we except those miraculous and isolated moments fate can bestow on a man, loving your work (unfortunately, the privilege of a few) represents the best, most concrete approximation of happiness on earth. But this is a truth not many know. This boundless region, the region of *le boulot*, the job, *il rusco*—of daily work, in other words—is less known than the Antarctic, and through a sad and mysterious phenomenon it happens that the people who talk most, and loudest, about it are the very ones who have never traveled through it. To exalt labor, in official ceremonies an insidious rhetoric is displayed, based on the consideration that a eulogy or a medal costs much less than a pay raise, and they are also more fruitful. There also exists a rhetoric on the opposite side, however, not cynical, but profoundly stupid, which tends to denigrate labor, to depict it as base, as if labor, our own or others', were something we could do without, not only in Utopia, but here, today; as if anyone who knows how to work were, by definition, a servant, and as if, on the contrary, someone who doesn't know how to work, or knows little, or doesn't want to, were for that very reason a free man. It is sadly true that many jobs are not lovable, but it is harmful to come on to the field charged with preconceived hatred. He who does this sentences himself, for life, to hating not only work, but also himself and the world. We can and must fight to see that the fruit of labor remains in the hands of those who work, and that work does not turn into punishment; but love or, conversely, hatred of work is an inner, original heritage, which depends greatly on the story of the individual and less than is believed on the productive structures within which the work is done.

As if he had caught the vibrations of my thinking, Faussone went on: "You know what my first name is? Tino, like lots of others. But my Tino is short for Libertino. When my father reported my birth he really wanted to call me Libero. The mayor, for all that he was a Fascist, was also a friend and would have let it go, but the Town Secretary couldn't be budged. These are all things my mother told me afterward. This Secretary said there was no Saint Libero, the name was too peculiar, and he didn't want to get into trouble. They would need permission from the provincial Fascist authorities, and maybe even from Rome. It was all nonsense, of course; the fact is that, to be on the safe side, he wanted to keep that little word Libero, 'free,' out of his ledgers. In the end there was nothing to be done; so, to make a long story short, my father fell back on Libertino, because, poor guy, he didn't realize it meant 'libertine.' He thought it was the same as when somebody's named Giovanni and they call him Giovannino. So Libertino I've remained, and anybody who happens to glance at my passport or my driver's license has a good laugh at my expense. Also because, year after year, going around the world as I do, I really did become a bit of a libertine, but that's another story, and besides you must've figured that out on your own. I'm a libertine, but it's not my specialty. That's not why I'm in this world, though if you were to ask me why I'm in this world, I'd have a hard time giving you an answer.

"My father wanted to call me Libero because he wanted me to be free. Not that he had any political ideas; his only idea about politics was not to make war because he had been through that. For him, free meant not having to work under a boss. Maybe twelve hours a day in your own shop all black with soot, and icy in the winter, like his was, or maybe as an emigrant, or going around with a wagon like the gypsies, but not under a boss, not in the factory, not making the same movements all your life, stuck on the assembly line until you're no good for anything else and they give you your severance pay and your pension and you sit on a park bench. That's why he didn't want me to go to Lancia, and secretly he would have liked me to stay in his shop and get married and have kids and teach them the job, too. Mind you, I'll say it right out: I do pretty well, but if my father hadn't insisted, sometimes nicely and sometimes not, on making me come to the shop with him after school to turn the crank of the forge and learn how from a three-millimeter plate he would make a half-sphere, true as truth, all by guesswork, without even a reference model, well, like I was saying, if I hadn't had that training in my father's shop, and if I had been satisfied with what they taught me in school, you can bet I'd be stuck on the assembly line right now."

We had come to a clearing, and Faussone pointed out to me some slight ridges, barely visible on the ground, the elegant labyrinths of moles, dotted by little conical mounds of fresh earth, expelled during their night shift. A short time before, he had taught me how to recognize larks' nests hidden in the depressions of the fields and had shown me an ingenious dormouse nest, in the form of a muff, half-concealed among the low branches of a larch. Later, he broke off his talk and stopped me, placing his left arm before my chest like a barrier. With his right hand he pointed to a slight quivering of the grass, a few steps from our path. A snake? No, on a stretch of packed earth a curious procession emerged: a hedgehog advanced cautiously, with brief pauses and resumptions, and behind him, or her, came five little ones, like tiny coaches drawn by a toy locomotive. The first was holding in his mouth the tail of the leader, and each of the others, in the same way, held on to the little tail of the one ahead of him. The guide stopped short at a big beetle, turned him on his back with one paw, and took him between his teeth. The little ones broke ranks and crowded around; then the leader drew back behind a bush, with all the others after him.

At dusk the clouded sky became clear; almost immediately we became aware of a distant, sad shrieking, and as often happens, we realized that we had already been hearing it, without giving it any thought. It was repeated at almost regular intervals, and there was no telling what direction it came from, but we then discovered, high above our heads, ordered flights of cranes, one after the other, in a long black line against the pale sky: it was as if they were weeping at being obliged to leave.

". . . but he lived to see me get out of the factory and start in this work I'm doing now, and I believe he was happy. He never said so to me, because he wasn't a man who talked much, but he had other ways of showing me, and when he saw that every now and then I was going off on a trip, he was surely envious, but with an honest man's envy, not like when you would want somebody else's luck and since you can't have it, you wish him all sorts of disasters. He would've liked a job like mine, even if the company makes money off you, because they don't take the result away from you: that stays there, it's yours, nobody can rob you of it. And he understood these things; you could tell by the way he stood there and looked at his stills, after he had finished them and shined them up. When the customers came to collect them, he would sort of give them a caress, and you could see he was sorry. If they weren't too far away, every now and then he would take his bicycle and go look at them, with the excuse that he was making sure they were working all right. And he would've liked this job also because of the traveling, because in his day you didn't get to travel much, so he had traveled very little, and badly. Talking about that year he spent in Savoie as an apprentice, he would say that all he remembered was the chilblains, the slaps, and the bad words they said to him in French. Then came Russia, the army, and you can imagine what kind of travel that was. On the other hand—and this will seem strange to you—the most beautiful year of his life, he told me several times, was right after the fall of Mussolini, the Badoglio government, when the Germans occupied everything, caught them at the Milan depot, disarmed them, packed them into cattle cars and shipped them to Germany to work. That surprises you, eh? But having a skill always comes in handy.

"The first months he had to tighten his belt a lot, but these aren't things I have to tell you about. He didn't want to sign up with Mussolini's Fascist Republic and come back to Italy that way. During the whole winter he worked with pick and shovel, and it was a terrible life, also because he had no clothes; he was still wearing his uniform. He had listed himself as a mechanic; he had just about given up all hope when, in March, they called him out of the ranks and set him to working in a shop as a plumber, and things there were already a little bit better. But then it turned out they were looking for engine drivers for the railroads, and he wasn't one, but he knew something about boilers, and besides he figured he could adapt to anything, and though he couldn't speak a word of German, he stepped forward, because when you're hungry, you get smart. He was lucky. They put him on coal locomotives, the kind that in the old days pulled freight trains and locals, and he got himself two girlfriends, one at either end of the line. Not that he was so venturesome, but he said it was easy; all the German men were in the army and the women ran after you. As you can imagine, he never came out and told the whole story, because when he was taken prisoner he was already married and also had a little kid, namely me; but on Sundays, when his friends would come by our house to drink a glass of wine, a word here, a grin there, half a sentence or so, and it wasn't hard to piece it together—also because I saw his friends laughing their heads off and my mother, with a hard face and a grim smile, would look away.

"And I understand him, because it was the one time in his life when he kind of escaped for a bit. Actually, if he hadn't found the German girlfriends, who were in the black market and gave him food, he might've ended up with TB like so many others, and my mother and I would've been in a bad way. As for driving the locomotive, he said it's easier than riding a bike: you just had to pay attention to the signals and put on the brakes if there was an air raid, drop everything, and run off into the fields. The only trouble was when fog came down, or else when there were alarms and the Germans made their own fog deliberately.

"To get to the point, when he reached the end of the line, instead of going to the railway dormitory, he would fill his pockets with coal, and his bag and his shirt, and give it all to the girl whose turn it was, because coal was all he had to give, and in return she would feed him supper, and in the morning he would be off again. After he had been going back and forth like this for a while, he found out that another Italian driver happened to work on the same line, another prisoner of war, a mechanic from Chivasso; but this other one drove the freights that traveled at night. The two of them met only now and then at one or the other end of the line, but since they came from neighboring towns, they made friends all the same. The man from Chivasso hadn't got himself organized and was starving because all he ate was what the railway gave him, so my father handed one of the girls over to him, gratis, just out of friendship; and after that the two men were always very close. When they both were home again, the Chivasso man used to come and visit us two or three times a year, and at Christmas he would bring us a turkey. Gradually, we all began to consider him kind of like a godfather to me, because in the meanwhile my real godfather, the one who made bushings for the Diatto factory, had died. In other words, he wanted to pay back, and in fact some years later he was the one who got me the job with Lancia and persuaded my father to let me go, and later he introduced me to the first firm where I worked as a rigger, though I didn't begin there as a rigger. He's still alive, and not all that old. He's on the ball; after the war he started raising turkeys and guinea fowl and made money.

"My father, on the other hand, went back to his old job, beating copper in his shop, a bang here, a bang there, always on the precise spot, so the sheet would all have the same thickness, and to smooth out the wrinkles, that he called *veje*, old women. He was offered good jobs in industry, especially in bodyworks, where the work wasn't all that different; my mother was on at him every day, to accept, because it was good money, and there was health insurance, pension, and all that. But he wouldn't even consider it; he said that the boss's bread has seven crusts, and it's better to be an eel's head than a sturgeon's tail: he was one of those men who talk in proverbs.

"By then tin-plated copper pots were out. Nobody wanted them, because you could buy aluminum pots in the store for less, and then came the stainless steel ones, and the kind with a special varnish so steaks won't stick, and there wasn't much money coming in, but he didn't feel like changing, so he started making autoclaves for hospitals, the things you sterilize instruments in for operations, also made of copper, but plated with silver instead of tin. That was when he and his friends got the idea I told you about, for the monument to the baker; and when it was rejected, he was sad and started drinking a bit more. He wasn't working all that much, because orders were scarce; and in his spare time he took to making other things, with a new shape, just for the pleasure of making them: shelves, flower vases. But he didn't sell them; he would set them aside or else give them away.

"My mother was a good woman, a churchgoer, but she didn't treat my father well. She never said anything to him, but she was tough, and you could see she didn't have great respect. She didn't realize that for this man, when his work ended, everything ended. He didn't want the world to change, and since the world does change, and nowadays changes fast, he didn't have the heart to keep up with it, and so he turned melancholy and listless. One day he didn't come home to lunch, and my mother found him dead in the shop, with his hammer in his hand, like he had always said."

WINE AND WATER

I HADN'T THOUGHT I would encounter such heat on the lower Volga at the end of September. It was Sunday, and the dormitory was uninhabitable; the Administratsya had installed a pathetic fan in each room, noisy and ineffectual, and the circulation of air depended entirely on the little corner window, the size of a newspaper page. I suggested to Faussone that we go to the river, walk down it until we reached a boat station, and then take the first boat that came along. He agreed, and we set off.

Along the towpath it was almost cool, and the sense of refreshment was enhanced by the unexpected transparency of the water and by its mossy, swampy odor. A faint breeze blew over the river's surface, wrinkling it in tiny waves, but at intervals the wind would change direction, and then from the land would come torrid gusts smelling of sun-baked clay. At the same time, under the newly calm surface of the water you could make out the confused features of some submerged, rustic houses. These weren't the result of remote events, Faussone explained: it hadn't been some divine punishment; nor were those houses a village of sinners. This was simply the effect of the gigantic dam that could be glimpsed beyond the bend in the river, built seven years ago; behind it a lake, or rather a sea, had collected, five hundred kilometers long. Faussone was as proud of the dam as if he had built it himself, whereas he had really only set up a crane. This crane, too, was the subject of a story: he promised to tell it to me one of these days.

We came to the station around nine. It was in two parts: one, a masonry construction on the shore; the other, of planks, practically a covered barge, floating on the water. And between the parts there was a gangway, jointed at the two ends. There was no one in sight. We stopped to consult a schedule, written in a neat hand, but full of erasures and corrections, pasted to the door of the waiting room. A short time later we saw a little old woman arriving, coming toward us with short, calm steps, not looking at us, because she was busy knitting a two-colored sweater. She passed us, found a folding chair in a corner, opened it, and sat down near the posted schedule, arranging the folds of her skirt beneath her. She went on knitting for a few moments; then she looked at us, smiled, and told us it was no use studying that schedule because it had expired.

Faussone asked her how long ago, and she answered vaguely: three days, or maybe even a week. And the new schedule hadn't been established yet, but the boats were running all the same. Where did we want to go? Embarrassed, Faussone replied that it made no difference to us; we would take whatever boat, so long as it came back by evening. We just wanted a bit of cool air and an outing on the river. The old woman nodded gravely and then supplied us with the valuable information that a boat would be coming along presently and would leave again immediately for Dubrovka. How far was that? Not far, an hour's journey, or maybe two hours, but what did we care? she asked us, with a radiant smile. Weren't we on vacation? Well, Dubrovka was just the place for us: there were woods, meadows; you could buy butter, cheese, and eggs; and a niece of hers also lived there. Did we want first-class tickets, or second? She was the ticket office.

We held council and decided on first class. The old woman

put down her knitting, disappeared through a little door, and reappeared at the window. She rummaged in a drawer and gave us the two tickets, which even for first class were very cheap. Crossing the flexible bridge we stepped onto the barge and waited. The barge was also deserted, but a little later a tall, thin young man arrived and sat down on the bench not far from us. He was dressed simply, with a worn jacket patched at the elbows, an open shirt. He had no baggage (nor did we, for that matter); he smoked one cigarette after another and observed Faussone with curiosity.

"Hmph. He must've realized we're foreigners," Faussone said. But after the third cigarette, the young man came over, greeted us, and spoke to us, naturally in Russian. After a brief exchange, I saw him grab Faussone's hand and shake it warmly, or rather, swing it vigorously in a circle, like the crank of an old car before they invented the starter.

"I swear I'd never have recognized him," Faussone said to me. "He's one of the workmen who helped me rig the crane for the dam, six years ago. But now that I think about it, I do seem to remember, because the cold was enough to crack stones and he didn't pay the slightest attention. He worked without any gloves and was dressed exactly like he is now."

The Russian seemed happy, as if he had found a lost brother; but Faussone, on the contrary, had not dropped his reserve and listened to the other man's wordy talk as if he were listening to a weather report on the radio. The man spoke in a rush, and I had a hard time following him, but I realized that in his speech the word *rasnitsa* recurred frequently, one of the few Russian words I know, which means "difference."

"It's his last name," Faussone explained to me. "That's actually what he's called: 'Difference.' And he's explaining to me that in the whole Lower Volga region he's the only one with that name. He must be a character."

Difference, after digging into all his pockets, pulled out a little ID card, all greasy and crumpled; and he showed me and Faussone that the photograph was really of him and that his name really was what he had said: Nikolai M. Rasnitsa. Immediately afterward, he declared that we were his friends, or rather his guests. In fact, by a lucky coincidence, that day was his birthday, and he was actually preparing to celebrate it with a river excursion. Fine, we would all go together to Dubrovka. He was awaiting the boat, and on it there would be two or three friends from his village who were also going to celebrate with him. To me, the thought of a Russian experience, a bit less formal than those connected with the job, was not unpleasant; but I saw a shadow of misgiving tinge Faussone's fàce, usually so inexpressive. And a little later, out of the side of his mouth, he whispered to me: "Things look bad."

The boat arrived, coming from the direction of the dam, and the two of us produced our tickets to be checked. Vexed, Difference told us we had made a big mistake buying tickets, especially first class and round trip. Weren't we his guests? He wanted to invite us on the outing, he was a friend of the captain and the whole crew, and on this line he never paid for a ticket, for himself or for his guests. We went on board; the boat, too, was deserted, except for Difference's two friends, seated on one of the benches on deck. They were a pair of giants, with jailbird faces the like of which I've never seen anywhere, in Russia or outside, except in some spaghetti Westerns. One was obese, and his trousers hung from a belt fastened tight below his belly; the other was thinner, with a pockmarked face, and his lower jaw stuck out so that his bottom teeth closed over the upper ones; this feature made him look like a mastiff, contradicting his eyes, also vaguely canine, but of a tender hazel color. Both men stank of sweat and were drunk.

The boat set off again. Difference explained to his friends who we were, and they said that was fine, the more the merrier. They made me sit between them, and Faussone sat beside Difference on the opposite bench. The fat man was carrying a package, wrapped in newspaper, carefully tied up with a string; he unwrapped it, and inside there were several rustic sandwiches filled with fatback. He passed them around, then he went somewhere below deck and came back up carrying a tin bucket by the handle, obviously a former paint can. From his pocket he extracted an aluminum cup, filled it with the liquid from the bucket, and invited me to drink. It was a sweet-ish, very strong wine, something like Marsala, but harsher, somehow edgy. To my taste it was decidedly bad, and I saw that also Faussone, who is a connoisseur, wasn't enthusiastic. But the two were indomitable: in the bucket there was at least three liters of wine, and they declared we had to finish it up during the outward trip; otherwise what kind of birthday would it be? And moreover, *niè strazno*, never fear: in Du-brovka we would find more, and even better.

In my scant Russian, I tried to defend myself: the wine was good, but this was enough for me, I wasn't used to drinking, I was seriously ill, bad liver, stomach. But there was nothing for it: the two, supported by Difference, produced a compulsive conviviality that bordered on menace, and I had to drink again and again. Faussone drank, too, but he was in less danger than I, because he can hold his wine, and also because, since his Rus-sian was better, he could make more articulate excuses or change the subject. He showed no signs of discomfort; he talked and drank; every now and then my eye, more and more clouded, would catch his clinical glance, but whether through distraction or a deliberate determination to be superior, he made no effort, throughout the trip, to come to my aid.

Wine has never agreed with me. That wine, in particular, plunged me into an unpleasant condition of humiliation and impotence. I had not lost lucidity, but I felt my ability to stand up gradually weakening, and thus I feared the moment when I would have to rise from the bench. I could feel my tongue growing thicker, and my visual field, especially, had irritatingly narrowed, and I witnessed the unfolding of the two banks of the river as if through a diaphragm, or rather as if my eyes were peering into a pair of those tiny opera glasses they used in the last century.

For all these combined reasons, I haven't retained a distinct memory of the trip. At Dubrovka things went a bit better; the wine was finished; there was a good, cool wind, with an odor of hay and stables; and after my first few hesitant steps, I felt reassured. Everybody seemed related in those parts: it turned out that the ticket seller's niece was the sister of the pockmarked friend, it was dinner time, and at all costs she wanted us to come along and eat with them. She and her husband lived near the river, in a tiny wooden house, painted a light blue, with fretwork doorways and window frames. In front of the house there was a little garden with green, yellow, and purple cabbages; and everything suggested a fairy dwelling.

The interior was scrupulously clean. The windows, and even the inside doors, were protected by net curtains from ceiling to floor, but the ceiling was no more than two meters high. On one wall, side by side, hung two cardboard ikons and, the same size, the photograph of a boy in uniform, his chest bedecked with medals. On the table was a sheet of oilcloth, with a steaming tureen on it; a great loaf of rye bread with a dark, wrinkled crust; four places set; and four hard-boiled eggs. The niece was a sturdy peasant of about forty, with rough hands and a sweet gaze; over her dark hair she wore a white kerchief knotted under her chin. Next to her sat her husband, an elderly man with short gray hair glued to his skull by the day's sweat; his face was gaunt and tanned, but his brow was pale. Opposite sat two blond boys, evidently twins, who seemed impatient to begin the meal but waited for their parents to swallow their first spoonful. Five more places had quickly been laid for us, so we were a bit crowded.

I wasn't hungry, but to avoid seeming rude, I tasted a bit of soup; our hostess scolded me with maternal severity, as she might treat a spoiled child. She wanted me to tell her why I "ate so badly." In a rapid aside, Faussone explained to me that in Russian to eat badly is like saying to eat scantily, just as in Italian we say to eat well rather than to eat a lot. I defended myself as best I could, with gestures, faces, halting words; and the hostess, more discreet than our two traveling companions, didn't insist.

The boat left again at about four. Besides our group, there was only one passenger on board, popping up from God knows where: a slight, ragged little man, with a short, sparse, untrimmed beard; of indefinite age, he had limpid, senseless eyes and a single ear; the other was reduced to an ugly, fleshy hole, from which a scar ran straight down to his chin. He was also a fraternal friend of Difference and the other two, and with us Italians he demonstrated an exquisite hospitality. He insisted on showing us over the boat from stem to stern, neglecting neither the hold, with its stifling fungus stink, nor the latrines, which I prefer not to describe. He appeared foolishly proud of every detail, which led us to deduce that he was either a retired sailor or perhaps a former shipyard worker, but he spoke with such an unusual accent, with such a prevalence of *o*'s over *a*'s, that even Faussone gave up asking him questions, since he wouldn't have understood the answers, in any case. His friends called him *Grafinya*, "Countess," and Difference explained to Faussone that the man really was a count and that, during the Revolution, he had escaped to Persia and had changed his name, but the story didn't seem clear to us, or convincing.

The heat had returned, and the left bank of the river, along which the boat was proceeding, was crowded with bathers. Mostly they were whole families, eating and drinking, wallowing in the water or roasting in the sun, stretched out on the dusty shore. Some of them, men and women, wore modest bathing suits that covered them from neck to knees; others were naked, and they moved about through the crowd with naturalness. The sun was still high: on board there was nothing to drink, not even water, and the sad wine of our companions was also finished. The Count had disappeared, and the other three were snoring, sprawled on the benches. I was thirsty, overheated. I suggested to Faussone that, once we were ashore, we should look for an isolated beach, undress, and have a swim ourselves.

Faussone was silent for a few minutes; then he answered crossly: "You know perfectly well I can't swim. I told you so that time I was telling you about the derrick and Alaska. And water makes me nervous. And you surely don't think I should learn here, in that water, which may be clean but is full of currents and undertow, and there isn't one lifeguard, and besides I'm not all that young.

"The fact is that when I was little nobody taught me, because around our parts there isn't any water for swimming in;

and the one time I did have a chance, it all went wrong. I had begun; I was learning on my own. I had the time and the will-power. and it went wrong. This was some years ago, in Calabria, when they were building the superhighway, and they sent me down there with the crane operator. I was to rig the laying-bridge, and he was to learn how to operate it. You don't know what a laying-bridge is? I didn't know either, at that time. It's a smart way of building reinforced concrete bridges, the kind that when you look at them they seem so simple, with rectangular piers and with beams set on top of them. The design is simple enough, but putting them up isn't so simple, like all top-heavy things, like bell-towers, and all. Obviously, building the pyramids of Egypt is another matter. Anyway, in my father's village there's a proverb that goes, 'Bridges and bell-towers: let your neighbors make them.' It rhymes, in our dialect.

"Well, just picture a fairly narrow valley, a road that has to cross it way up high, and the piers already made, figure about fifty meters apart. You know, the central ones might even be sixty or seventy meters high, so there's no question of hoisting the beams up with a crane, not to mention the fact that you can't always count on the terrain down below; and in this place I'm telling you about, in Calabria, that is, there wasn't anything, it was the mouth of one of those streams where there's water only when it rains—in other words almost never—but when there is water, it carries away everything. A scree of sand and boulders: absolutely impossible to set up a crane there. The middle pier was already a few meters out in the sea. And you also have to imagine a beam, not one of those toothpick things, but a great shaft about as long as Corso Stupinigi is wide, weighing maybe a hundred or even a hundred and fifty tons. And it's not that I don't trust cranes, because that's my business after all; but a crane that will lift a hundred tons to a height of seventy meters has yet to be invented. Instead, they invented the laying-bridge.

"I don't have a pencil handy now, but you have to picture a long dolly, so long that it can only be assembled on the spot, and this, in fact, was the job I was supposed to do. To be precise, it had to be long enough so that it would always rest on at least three piers. In this case, counting also the thickness of the piers, it comes to a bit less than a hundred and fifty meters. There you are: a laying-bridge; and they call it that because it's used to lay the beams. Inside the structure there are two tracks, running its whole length. On the tracks run two smaller dollies, and each of them carries a winch. The beam is on the ground, anywhere below the track: the two winches pull it inside the structure; then the laying-bridge starts moving, very slowly, like a caterpillar, and it moves on some rollers that are set on the head of the piers. It moves with the beam inside, and it reminds you of a pregnant animal, as it moves from pier to pier until it reaches the right position, and there the winches turn backward, and the laying-bridge gives birth to the beam. That is, it lowers it precisely into its sockets. I've seen it done, and it was a beautiful job, the kind that gives satisfaction because you can see the machines working smoothly, without straining and without any noise. For that matter, I don't know why, but seeing huge things move slowly and quietly, like, for example, a ship setting out, has always had an effect on me, and not only on me. Other people have told me the same thing. Then when the real bridge is finished, you dismantle the laying-bridge, load it onto trucks, and carry it away to be used somewhere else.

"What I've been telling you is the ideal, I mean the way the job should have gone, whereas, on the contrary, it got off to a bad start right away. I won't go into detail, but every minute there was a ballsup, beginning with the steel structures I was supposed to assemble, the segments of the laying-bridge I was telling you about. They didn't meet specifications, and we had to file them all down, one by one. You can bet I complained; in fact, I dug in my heels. It would be a fine thing if a man had to pay for other people's mistakes, and a rigger had to wield a saw and a file. I went to the local foreman and I spoke my mind: all the parts had to be precise, lined up, in order, on the spot; or else no Faussone; they could find themselves another one somewhere in the Calabrias. Because in this world, if you let a person walk over you once, then that's the end."

I kept feeling the water's lure, constantly renewed by the splash of the little waves against the keel, and by the happy cries of the Russian children, blond, sturdy, and radiant, as they swam after one another or dived in like otters. I failed to understand the correlation between the laying-bridge and Faussone's rejection of water and swimming, and I cautiously asked him about it.

Faussone scowled. "You never let me tell a thing my own way." And he withdrew into a frowning silence. The reproach seemed (and still seems) completely undeserved to me, because I have always let him talk as he wanted and as long as he wanted, and for that matter the reader is my witness. But now I kept my mouth shut, out of love of peace. Our double silence was dramatically interrupted. On the next bench, Mr. Difference woke up, stretched, looked around with a smile, and began to undress. When he was in his shorts, he woke up his fat friend and handed him the bundle of his clothes, waved to us politely, climbed over the railing, and jumped into the river. With a few vigorous strokes, he was beyond the pull of the screw; then, swimming quite calmly on his side, he headed for a little cluster of white houses, from which a wooden jetty extended. The fat man immediately went back to sleep, and Faussone resumed his story.

"There. You see? Well, it makes me mad, because I'd never be able. I could never do a thing like that. And the laying-bridge and swimming do have a connection; you just have to be patient and the connection will be clear. I have to tell you, being around a work site is something I enjoy, provided everything runs the way it should, but that foreman got on my nerves, because he was the type that doesn't give a damn, so long as his paycheck comes at the end of the month, and these guys don't realize that if you stop giving a damn for too long maybe the check will stop coming, for you and for everybody else. He was little, with flabby hands, and he used brilliantine on his hair, which had a part down the middle. He was blond, didn't even look like a Calabrian, but he was a little rooster, so proud of himself. And since he answered me back, I told him it was all right with me: if there was no cooperation, that suited me fine, too. The weather was beautiful, there was the sun, the sea was right nearby, I'd never had a vacation at the beach, so all right, I was taking a holiday until he had all the parts of my structure ready for me, from the first to the last. I called the firm, and since it suited them as well, they immediately said yes. And I think I did things the right way, didn't I?

"For my vacation I didn't stir from that place, out of spite, because I wanted to keep an eye on the job, and because there was no need to move anyway. I found a room in a little house not a hundred meters from the concrete piers. A family lived there, nice people; in fact, I was thinking about them just now, in Dubrovka, while we were having dinner, because good people are alike all over, and besides everybody knows that between Russians and Calabrians there isn't much difference. They were nice, clean, respectful, good-humored; the husband had a funny job: he mended holes in fish-nets. The wife kept house and tended the garden, and the little boy didn't do anything, but he was a good kid all the same. I didn't do anything, either. At night I slept like a king, in a silence where you could hear only the waves of the sea, and during the day I would sunbathe like a tourist, and I got it into my head that this was the right moment to learn how to swim.

"I told you before, down there I had everything I could need. I had all the time in the world, there was nobody to watch me or disturb me or make fun of me because I was learning to swim when I was almost thirty; the sea was calm, there was a pretty little beach to rest on, and no rocks on the bottom, just a fine white sand, smooth as silk, sloping down very gradually so you could go out almost a hundred meters and still touch bottom; the water only came up to your shoulders. All the same, I have to confess I was scared to death: not with fear in my head—I don't know if I can explain this—but with fear in my belly and in my knees, the kind of fear animals have, in other words. But I'm also hardheaded, as you've noticed already, so I made a schedule for myself. First thing, I had to get rid of my fear of the water. Then I had to convince myself I could stay afloat: everybody does, even children, even animals; why shouldn't I? And, finally, I was to learn to move forward. I had everything I needed, including this schedule, and still I didn't feel easy the way a man on his vacation should. I felt like I had something itching me inside; it was all kind of mixed up together: my worry about the work that wasn't proceeding, and also another fear, the kind a man feels when he's made up his mind to do a certain thing and then isn't able to do it and he loses his self-confidence, so he'd have been better off not even starting, but since he's hardheaded he starts all the same. Now I've changed some, but that's the way I was then.

"Overcoming the fear of water was the worst job; in fact, I have to confess I didn't overcome it at all. I just got used to it. It took me two days. I would go into the water till it was up to my chest; I would take a deep breath, hold my nose, then put my head under water. The first times it was death: I mean it; I felt like I was dying. I don't know if we all have it, but I have sort of an automatic mechanism: the minute I put my head under, all the shutters came down in my throat. I felt the water inside my ears, and it seemed to be flowing down those two little channels into my nose, down my gullet, into the lungs, until it would drown me. So I was forced to stand up, and I almost felt like thanking the Almighty for dividing the water from the dry land, like the Bible says. It wasn't even fear: it was horror, like when you suddenly see a dead body and your hair all stands on end. But I mustn't get ahead of myself; and, to make it short: I got used to it.

"Staying afloat, the next thing, I saw was somewhat complicated. Various times I had seen how others do, when they play dead. I tried it, too, and I floated, no question about that. But to keep floating, I had to fill my lungs with air, like those pontoons in Alaska I told you about; and a man can't keep his lungs full all the time. The moment comes when you have to exhale, and then I felt myself sinking, like the pontoons when it was time to tow them away. And so I had to kick my legs in the water as fast as I could, still holding my breath, until I touched bottom. Then I would stand up, panting like a dog, and I would want to give the whole thing up. But you know how it is when you face an obstacle, and it's like you had made a bet and you hate to lose: that's how it was with me. And for that matter, it's the same on the job; maybe I walk out on an easy job, but never on a hard one. The trouble all comes from the fact that we have our airpipes in the wrong place. Dogs and, even more, seals have them in the right place, and they swim from the time they're pups without any fuss, and with nobody teaching them. So I resigned myself, for this first time, to learn to swim on my back. I would have been satisfied with that, though it didn't seem so natural to me; but if you stay on your back in the water you have your nose in the air and so, theoretically, you can breathe. At the beginning I took short breaths, to keep from emptying the pontoons too much, then I revved up, a bit at a time, until I was convinced that you could also breathe without sinking, or at least without submerging your nose, which is the most important part. But all it took was a little wave no higher than this and I was scared again and lost my bearings.

"I made all my experiments, and when I felt tired or out of breath I would go ashore and stretch out to sunbathe near the superhighway pier. I had driven a nail into it, for hanging up my clothes; otherwise, they'd have been full of ants. I told you, those piers were about fifty meters high, maybe more; they were bare concrete, still with the marks of the mold. About two meters above the ground there was a stain, and the first few times I didn't even pay any attention to it. One night it rained, and the spot turned darker, but I didn't pay any attention that time, either. To be sure, it was a funny spot. It was the only one; all the rest of the pier was clean, and so were the other piers. It was a meter long, divided into two parts, one shorter than the other. It looked like an exclamation point, only a little slanted."

He was silent for a time, rubbing his hands as if he were washing them. We could hear distinctly the throb of the engine and could already discern the boat station in the distance.

"Listen. I don't like telling lies. Exaggerate a little, yes, specially when I'm telling about my work; and I don't believe that's a sin, because anybody who listens to me catches on immediately. Well, one day I realized that along that stain there was a crack, and a procession of ants was going in and out. I got curious. I hit the pier with a rock and I heard a hollow sound. I hit it harder, and the concrete, which was only an inch thick, crumbled, and inside there was a skull.

"It was like they had shot me between the eyes; and I actually did lose my balance, but there he was, all right, and he was looking at me. Just after that I got some funny disease: scabs appeared here at my waist, and they itched, and when they dropped off, more came. But I was almost glad, because they gave me a good excuse to drop the whole job and go home. So I didn't learn to swim, then or later, because every time I go into the water, whether it's the ocean or a river or a lake, I begin to get nasty thoughts."

THE BRIDGE

ON THE OTHER HAND, when they offered me a job in India, I wasn't all that inclined. Not that I knew much about India. You know how easy it is to get a mistaken notion of a country, and since the world is big, and it's all made up of different countries, and practically speaking, you can't visit all of them, you end up with a head full of crazy ideas about all countries, maybe even including your own. All I knew about India I can tell you in a few words: they have too many babies; they starve to death because it's against their religion to eat cows; they killed Gandhi because he was too good; the country's bigger than Europe and they speak God knows how many languages, and so, for want of anything better, they settled on English; and then there's the story of Mowgli the Frog that, when I was a kid, I thought was real. Oh, I was forgetting the Kamasutra business and the hundred and thirty-seven ways of making love, or maybe it's two hundred and thirty-seven. I don't remember exactly any more, I read it once in a magazine while I was waiting to get my hair cut.

"In other words, I would almost rather have stayed in Turin.

I was in Via Lagrange in those days, living with those two
aunts of mine; sometimes instead of going to a pensione I visit
them, because they make a fuss over me, cook special dishes,
in the morning they get up without a sound so as not to wake
me, and they go to the early Mass and buy me fresh rolls still
hot from the oven. They have only one fault: they want me to
get married, and that in itself wouldn't be so bad, but they're
kind of heavy-handed about it, and they keep introducing me
to girls who aren't exactly my type. I've never figured out
where the old ladies find them: maybe in convent schools.
They're all alike: they seem made of wax, when you talk to
them they don't dare even look you in the face, they make me
terribly embarrassed, I don't know where to begin, and I get
as tongue-tied as they are. So it may happen that, other times,
when I come to Turin, I don't even get in touch with my
aunts, and I go straight to the pensione; also to keep from dis-
turbing them.

"Like I was saying, that was a time when I was kind of tired
of roving around, and in spite of this mania of my aunts' I
would gladly have stayed put; but at the office, they poured it
on, they know my weak spot, and they know how to twist me
around their finger: it was such an important job, and if I
didn't go they couldn't think of anyone else to send. What
with one thing and another, they telephoned me every day,
and besides, like I said before, I can't keep the engine idling,
and I can take the city only for a short while, so the fact is
that in late February I began to think it's better to wear out
shoes than sheets, and at the beginning of March I was at
Fiumicino climbing into a Boeing, all yellow, Air Pakistan.

"The trip was a laugh from beginning to end: I mean I was
the only serious traveler. Half were German and Italian tourists, all keyed up from the start at the idea of going to see Indian dance because they thought it was belly dancing, whereas
I actually saw it and it's very prim: they dance just with the
eyes and the fingers. The other half, on the contrary, were
Pakistani workers going home from Germany, with their wives
and little kids, and they were happy, too, because they were
on their way home and it was their vacation. There were also

some women workers; in fact, in the seat next to mine there was a girl in a purple sari. A sari is that dress they wear without sleeves, without any front or back. This girl, I was saying, she was a beauty; I don't know how to describe her: she looked like she was transparent, and with a kind of glow inside, and she had eyes that talked. Too bad she talked only with her eyes; I mean she only spoke Indian and some German. And I've never wanted to learn German; otherwise, I would gladly have struck up a conversation, and I swear it would have been livelier than my conversations with those girls my aunts dig up; no offense, but they're all as flat as if Saint Joseph had run his plane over them. Well, enough about that. Besides, I don't know if this happens with you, too; but with me, the more foreign a girl is, the more she appeals to me, because there's the curiosity.

"The perkiest in the bunch were the kids. There was a full house and a half, and there wasn't room for them all to sit down; on those airlines I believe they don't even charge for kids. They were barefoot and chattering among themselves like a flock of sparrows, and they played hide and seek under the seats, so every now and then one would pop up between your legs, flash you a little smile, and skitter off again. When the plane was over the Caucasus there were some air pockets, and a lot of the grown-up passengers were afraid, and some were sick. But the kids, on the contrary, invented a new game: the minute the plane veered to the left and tilted a bit, they would let out a yell all together and run to the windows on the left hand side; and then the same on the right side, until the pilot realized how the plane was swerving, and at first he couldn't figure it out and thought something had gone wrong; then he caught on to what the kids were doing and he called the hostess to make them stay put. The hostess was the one who told me about this, because it was a long trip and we struck up an acquaintance. She was beautiful, too, and had a pearl stuck into one nostril. When she brought the supper tray, there was nothing but white and yellow pastes. They were disgusting, but what the hell: I ate them all, because she was looking at me and I didn't want to seem finicky.

"You know how it is when they're about to land, the engines slow down a little; the plane tilts forward, and it seems like a big, tired bird; then it moves down lower and lower, until you can see the lights of the field, and when the flaps are raised and the ailerons come out, the whole plane shakes, and it's as if the air had become bumpy. It was the same this time, too, but it was a troublesome landing. Obviously the tower wasn't giving permission, so we began circling; and whether there was turbulence or whether the pilot was green, or there was something wrong, the plane rattled like it was riding over the teeth of a saw; and through the window you could see the wings flapping like a bird's, or like they were on hinges; and this went on for about twenty minutes. Not that I was worried, because I know this happens sometimes, but it came back to me later when I saw what happened to the bridge. Anyway, we landed somehow or other, the engines died, and they opened the exits. Well, when they opened them, instead of air, it seemed like warm water poured into the cabin, with a special smell, which is actually the smell you smell everywhere in India: a heavy odor, a mixture of incense, cinnamon, sweat, and rot. I didn't have much time to waste, I collected my suitcase and ran to catch the little Dakota that was to take me to the work site, and luckily it was almost dark because one look at the plane was enough to scare you; and then, when it took off, even if you couldn't see it, it scared you still worse, but by that time there was nothing to be done, and anyway it was a short trip. It was like those cars in old comic movies; but I saw that the others were all calm, so I kept calm, too.

"I was calm, and pleased, because I was almost there, and because it was a matter of doing a job that suited me. I still haven't told you: it was a big job, rigging a suspension bridge, and I've always thought that bridges are the most beautiful work there is, because you're sure they'll never do anybody harm; in fact, they do good, because roads pass over bridges, and without roads we would still be like savages. In other words, bridges are sort of the opposite of boundaries, and boundaries are where wars start. Well, that's how I thought about bridges, and actually I still think like that; but after I worked on that bridge in India, I began to think I would also have liked to study more. If I had studied, I would likely have become an engineer; but if I was an engineer, the last thing I'd do would be to design a bridge, and the last bridge I'd design would be a suspension bridge."

I pointed out to Faussone that what he was saying seemed somewhat contradictory to me, and he agreed that it was, but before passing judgment I should wait till the end of his story: it often happens that a thing can be good in general and bad in particular, and that is exactly how it was in this case.

"The Dakota landed in a way I'd never seen before, and I've done a lot of flying. When it was in sight of the field, the pilot came down till he was grazing the strip, but instead of slowing down, he gunned the engines to the maximum, making the devil's own racket. He flew over the whole field at an altitude of two or three meters, he zoomed up just over the sheds, made a low turn, and then landed, bouncing three or four times like when you skip a flat stone over a stretch of water. They explained to me that it was to chase off the vultures, and in fact I had seen them, while the plane was coming down, in the beam of the searchlights; but I hadn't realized what they were. They looked like huddled-up old women, but later I wasn't amazed, because in India a thing always looks like something else. In any case, it's not that they were scared off: they shifted a little, hopping with half-opened wings, not even taking flight, and as soon as the plane stopped, they gathered all around it like they were waiting for something, and every now and then one of them would take a quick peck at the next one. They're really ugly animals.

"But there's no point in me telling you about India, there'd be no end to it, and you may even have been there. . . . You haven't? Anyhow, these are all things you can read in books; but how you draw the cables of a suspension bridge isn't in any book, or at least not the impression it makes on you. So we arrived at the work site's airport, which was only a field of packed earth, and they sent us to sleep in the dormitory. It wasn't all that uncomfortable, except that it was hot. But this heat business is another thing I don't have to go into. Just assume it was hot all the time, day and night, and down there you sweat so much that, excuse the expression, you don't have to go to the bathroom. I mean, all through this story it was hot as damnation, and I won't keep repeating that or I'd be wasting time.

"The next morning I went to the site manager to introduce myself. He was an Indian engineer, and we spoke English, and we understood each other fine, because the Indians, if you ask me, speak English better than the English, or at least it's more clear. The English just don't have an inkling, they talk fast and chew all their words, and if you don't understand, they seem surprised, but they don't make any effort. Well, he explained the job to me, and first off he gave me like a little veil to put under my helmet, because down there they have malaria, and in fact at the windows of the buildings there were mosquito nets. I saw that the Indian workers on the site didn't wear the veil, and I asked him, and he replied that they all had malaria already.

"The engineer was very worried. I mean, in his place I would have been worried: but he, even if he was, it didn't show. He spoke very calmly and told me that they had hired me to draw the supporting cables of the suspension bridge, that the bulk of the work was done, namely they had already deepened the bed of the river in five places, where the five piers were to be made; and it had been a lousy job, because that river carries a lot of sand, even when it's low, and so the excavations kept filling up as fast as they were dug. And then they sunk the caissons and sent miners down inside, to dig out the rock, and two of the men had drowned, but in the end they sank the caissons, filled them with gravel and cement, and the dirty part of the job was over, finally. Listening to him, I began to get worried myself, because he mentioned the two dead men casually, like it was something natural, and I began to get the idea that this was a place where you'd better not count on other people being careful, and you'd better be double-careful yourself.

"I was telling you in that engineer's place I wouldn't have been quite so calm. About two hours earlier they had phoned him to say that something incredible was happening, namely, that now the piers were finished, a flood was on its way and the river was flowing in a different direction. He told me this like another person would have said the roast was burned. He really must've had slow reactions. Another Indian arrived with a turban and a jeep, and the engineer said very politely that we'd get together again some other time and now he was very sorry. But I realized he was going to have a look, and I asked to go with him. He made a face I didn't understand, but he said yes. I don't know; maybe because he had respect, maybe because you never turn down an offer of advice, or maybe it was just out of politeness. He was very polite, but the kind of man who lets things take their course. He also had imagination: as we were riding in the jeep—and I won't bother to tell you about the road—instead of thinking about the flood, he told me how they had managed to throw walkways across the river (he called them catwalks, but I don't think any intelligent cat would have walked over them; I'll tell you about them later, anyway). Another man would have taken a boat or would have fired a harpoon like the ones they use for whales; but this guy sent for all the kids of the village there and offered a prize of ten rupees for the one who could fly a kite over to the opposite side. One kid did it, the engineer paid him the reward (and he wasn't throwing his money around, because that's about three dollars), then he had a thicker rope knotted to the kite string, and so on, until they got to the steel cables of the catwalk. He had just finished telling this story when we reached the bridge, and the sight took his breath away, too.

"Here at home we don't think much about the power of rivers. At that point, the river was seven hundred meters wide, and it made a bend. To me it didn't seem all that smart to put the bridge just there, but apparently it couldn't be avoided, because an important railway line had to go over it. You could see the five piers in the midst of the current, and further on, the approach piers, shorter and shorter, to connect with the plain. On the five big piers, the support towers were already in place, fifty meters high; and between two of the piers there was already a service structure, laid on its side, a light, temporary bridge, in other words, for the final span to be set on. We were on the right bank, which was buttressed by a concrete embankment, nice and strong, but there the river had vanished: during the night it had begun to eat at the left bank, where there was an identical buttress, and early that morning the river had broken through it.

"Around us there were maybe a hundred Indian workers, and they didn't bat an eye. They were calmly looking at the river, sitting on their heels, the way they do. I wouldn't last five minutes, and I don't know how they manage; obviously they were taught as children. When they saw the engineer, they stood up for a minute and greeted him, putting their hands to their chest, this way, folded, like they were going to pray. They made a little bow, then sat down again. We were too low to see the situation clearly, so we climbed the ladder of the tower on the bank, and then we could really take in the whole show.

"Below us, I told you, there was no water any more, just some black mud that was already beginning to steam and stink under the sun, and in it was a big mess of uprooted trees, planks, empty drums, and dead animals. The water was all running against the left bank, like it wanted to carry it off, and in fact, while we were standing there in a daze, watching, not knowing what to do or what to say, we saw a chunk of the embankment come loose, about ten meters long, and slam against one of the piers, bounce back and then swirl down on the current, like it was wood, not concrete. The water had already carried off a good part of the left bank; it had penetrated the breach and was flooding the fields on the other side: it had made a round lake more than a hundred meters across, and more water, like a mean animal bent on doing harm, kept pouring into it, spinning because of the thrust behind it, and spreading out before our eyes.

"The stream brought down all sorts of things: not only flotsam, but what seemed floating islands. Obviously, upstream the river passed through a wood, because trees were coming down with their leaves and roots, and even whole hunks of shore,

and you couldn't figure out how they kept afloat, with grass
on them, earth, trees still standing or else on their side, patches
of landscape, in other words. They traveled at top speed;
sometimes they slipped between the piers and sped away on
the other side; sometimes they bumped against the bases and
broke into two or three pieces. You could see that the piers
were really solid, because a kind of tangle had formed against
the bases: planks, branches, trunks. And you could see the
force of the water, piling against it and unable to dislodge
them; and it made a strange racket, like thunder, but underground.

"I tell you, I was glad he was the engineer; but if I had been
in his place, I think I would have made myself a little busier.
Not that much could be done there and then, but I had the
impression that, if he obeyed his instincts, he would sit on his
heels, too, like his workers, and stay there watching till God
knows when. It seemed rude for me to give him advice, me
who had just arrived, and him the engineer; but it was plain as
the nose on your face that he didn't know which way to turn,
and he paced up and down the bank without opening his
mouth, and, in other words, he was spinning his wheels, so I
plucked up my nerve and told him that in my opinion it would
be a good thing to send for some stones, some boulders, the
biggest they could get, and throw them down on the left bank,
but sort of quick, because while we were standing there talking, the river had carried off, at one whack, two more slabs of
the embankment, and the whirlpool in the lake had started
whirling faster than ever. We started to get into the jeep, and
at that very moment we saw a mass of trees coming down,
with earth and branches, the whole thing, and I'm not exag-
gerating, big as a house, and it was rolling like a ball. It stuck
into the span where there was the service structure and bent it
like a straw and pulled it down into the water. There really
wasn't much to be done; the engineer told the workers to go
home, and we also went back to the camp to telephone for the
stones; but along the way the engineer told me, still very calm,
that all around that area there was nothing but fields, black
earth, and mud, and if I wanted a stone the size of a walnut, I

would have to travel at least a hundred miles to find one: like stones were a craving of mine, the kind women get when they're expecting. In other words, he was a polite character, but strange; he seemed to be playing rather than working, and he got on my nerves.

"He started telephoning somebody or other; I think it was a government office. He talked Indian, and I couldn't understand any of it, but it sounded like first came the operator, then the secretary's secretary, then the real secretary, and the man he wanted never came, and in the end they were cut off, a bit like home, in other words; but he didn't lose his temper and began again from the beginning. Between secretaries he told me, however, that in his opinion there wouldn't be anything useful for me to do at the site there for some days. I could stay if I liked, but he advised me to take the train and go to Calcutta, and so I went. I didn't clearly understand if he was giving me this advice to be polite or to get rid of me. In any case, I didn't profit much. To tell you the truth, he warned me not even to try to find a hotel room; he gave me the address of a private house, and I was to go there because they were friends of his, and I would be comfortable with them, also from the hygienic point of view.

"I won't tell you about Calcutta. I was there five days, a waste of time. There are more than five million inhabitants and terrible poverty, and you see it right off. Imagine, the minute I came out of the station, and it was evening, I saw a family going to bed, and they were going to sleep inside a length of cement pipe, a new one, the kind they use for sewers, four meters long, one meter diameter. There was the Papa, the Mama, and three kids. They had put a little lamp in the pipe, and two pieces of cloth, one at one end, one at the other; and they were lucky because most people slept on the sidewalk, wherever.

"The engineer's friends, it turned out, weren't Indians; they were Parsees. He was a doctor, and I got along with them fine. When they found out I was Italian they made a big fuss over me; God only knows why. I didn't know what Parsees are, or even that they exist, and to tell you the truth even now

I'm not quite clear on them. Maybe you, belonging to a different religion, can explain to me—"

I had to disappoint Faussone; I knew practically nothing about the Parsees, except their macabre funerals, where, to make sure the corpse won't pollute earth, water, or fire, it isn't buried or submerged or cremated, but left for the vultures to consume in the Towers of Silence. But I supposed these towers no longer existed, and hadn't since the days of Salgari's exotic tales.

"That's what you think! They exist, all right; the couple told me about them. They weren't churchgoers, though, and they said that when they die they'll have themselves buried in the regular way. The towers still exist: not in Calcutta, but in Bombay. There are four of them, each with its crew of vultures, but they only operate four or five times a year. Well, they were telling me something new. A German engineer came with a lot of leaflets, he got himself introduced to the Parsee priests, and he told them how German technicians had designed a grille to be placed at the bottom of the towers: a grille of electric resistors that would burn the dead body very slowly without flames, without smell, and without contaminating anything. It would take a German, wouldn't it? Anyway, the priests started arguing and apparently they're arguing still, because they have progressives and conservatives, too. The doctor was laughing while he told me this story, and his wife spoke up and said that in her opinion nothing will come of it, not for religious reasons but because of kilowatt-hours and the local administration.

"In Calcutta everything is cheap, but I didn't dare buy anything, or even go to the movies, because of the filth and the infections. I stayed at home and chatted with the Parsee lady, who was full of education and sense—in fact, I must remember to send her a card—and she explained to me all about India, and you could go on forever. But I was on tenterhooks, and every day I telephoned to the site, but either the engineer was out or he wouldn't come to the phone. Then I caught him on the fifth day and he told me I might as well come back, the river was down, and the work could be started; and so I went.

"I reported to the engineer, who still looked like his mind was somewhere else; and I found him in the midst of the yard where the sheds were, with about fifty men around him, and it seemed like he was waiting for me. He said hello in their way, with his hands to his chest, and then he introduced me to the gang: 'This is Mr. Peraldo, your Italian foreman.' They all bowed, with their hands pressed together, and I stood there like a dope. I thought he had forgotten my name, because you know how foreigners always have trouble with names, and to me, for that matter, it seemed like all Indians were named Singh, and I figured the same thing must've happened to him. I told him I was Faussone, not Peraldo, and he gave me this angelic smile and said, 'Sorry, but you know, all you Europeans look alike.' In other words, it gradually came out that this engineer, whose name was Chaitania, screwed things up not only on the job but also when it came to names. And this Mr. Peraldo wasn't somebody he had dreamed up: Peraldo really existed; he was a master mason from Biella, who, by coincidence, was also supposed to arrive that morning, and he was in charge of anchoring the cables of the bridge. And he actually did arrive a little later, and I was glad, because meeting somebody from your own country is always a pleasure. How the engineer managed to take me for him and say we looked alike is one of life's mysteries, because I'm tall and thin and Peraldo was dumpy; I was about thirty, and he would never see fifty again; he had a little Charlie Chaplin mustache, and even then the only hair I had on my head was this little patch back here. In other words, if we looked anything alike, it was only the way we bent our elbows, because he also enjoyed eating and drinking well, and down there it wasn't all that easy.

"Meeting a mason from Biella in such an out-of-the-way place didn't surprise me all that much, because if a man roams the world, wherever he goes he finds a Neapolitan who makes pizza and a Biellese who makes walls. Once I met a Biellese in Holland on a job, and he said that God made the world, except for Holland, which was made by the Dutch, but the Dutch, for the dikes, had called in masons from Biella, because nobody has yet invented a machine that will build walls. And it seemed a nice saying to me, even if nowadays it isn't all that true any more. This Peraldo I was lucky to run into, because he had roamed the world much worse than me, and he knew a thing or two, even if he didn't talk much; and also because, I don't know how he had managed, in the dormitory he had a good supply of Nebiolo, and every now and then he would offer me a drink. He would offer me a little, not much, because he too wasn't exactly openhanded and he didn't want to make a dent in his capital. But he was right, too, because the job dragged on and on, and here I really have to say it's the same the world over; jobs finished by the deadline in the specifications are something I haven't seen much of.

"He took me to see the tunnels for the anchorages: because the cables of that bridge, you understand, would be under big tension, and then the usual anchorages aren't enough. The cables had to be fixed in a block of concrete, made like a wedge and set in an inclined tunnel dug out of the cliff. There were four tunnels, two for each cable. But what tunnels! They were like caverns. I'd never seen anything of the kind before: eighty meters long, ten meters wide at the mouth and fifteen at the back, with a rake of thirty degrees. . . . No, no, don't make that face, because you're going to write these things down afterward, and I wouldn't want mistakes to get printed, or at least—excuse me for saying so—not through my fault."

I promised Faussone I would be very careful to follow his indications, and under no circumstances would I yield to the professional temptation to invent, embellish, and expand; and therefore I would add nothing to his report, though I might pare away a little, as the sculptor does when he carves the form from the block. And Faussone declared himself in agreement. So, carving from the great block of details he supplied me, in some disorder, I discerned the emerging form of a long, slender bridge, supported by five towers made of boxes of steel, and hung from four festoons of steel cable. Each festoon was 170 meters long, and each of the two cables consisted of a monstrous braid of eleven thousand individual strands, each five millimeters in diameter.

"I already told you the other evening how for me every job is like a first love; but this time I caught on right away that the love was a real involvement, the kind that if you end up in one piece you can consider yourself lucky. Before beginning, I spent a week, like I was in school, taking lessons from the engineers. There were six of them, five Indians and one from the company: four hours every morning with a notebook for taking notes, and then all afternoon studying them, because it was really like the work of a spider, only spiders are born already knowing their job, and besides, if they fall, they don't have far to fall and they don't do themselves much harm because they have a built-in lifeline. For that matter, after this job I'm telling you about, every time I see a spider in his web I remember my eleven thousand strands, I mean twenty-two thousand, because there were two cables; and I feel like I'm sort of a relative of his, specially when the wind's blowing.

"Then it was my turn to teach the lesson to my men. They were genuine Indians, not like those Alaskans I told you about before. At first, I have to confess I didn't have much confidence, seeing them sitting around me on their heels, or some with their legs folded and their knees sticking out, like the statues on their churches I saw in Calcutta. They would stare at me, never ask any questions. But then, a bit at a time, I dealt with them one by one, and I saw they hadn't missed a word; and if you ask me, they're more intelligent than we are, or maybe it's because they were afraid of losing their job, because down there they don't pull their punches. They're men like us, after all, even if they have a turban and don't wear shoes and every morning, no matter what, they spend two hours praying. They also have their problems; there was one with a sixteen-year-old son who was already shooting dice and his father was worried because the boy always lost; another one had a sick wife; and another had seven children, but he said he didn't agree with the government and didn't want the operation, because he and his wife liked kids, and he also showed me their picture. They were really beautiful, and his wife was beautiful, too. All Indian girls are beautiful, but Peraldo, who had been in India for quite a while, explained to me that there was nothing doing with them. He also said that it's different in the city, but there are certain diseases in circulation that it's best to steer clear of. In other words, to conclude: I've never done the fasting I did that time in India. But back to the job.

"I told you about the catwalks, and about the trick with the kite to draw the first strand. Obviously, they couldn't fly twenty-two thousand kites. To draw the cables of a suspension bridge into place there's a special system: you set up a winch, and six or seven meters above each catwalk you install an endless cable, like one of those old belts, stretched between two pulleys, one on each bank. To the endless cable you attach an idle pulley, with four grooves; inside each groove you pass a loop of the single strand, which comes from a big spool. And then you start the pulleys and you draw the idle pulley from one bank to the other. That way, with one trip you draw eight wires. The workmen, apart from those who set up the loops and those who remove them, stand on the catwalk, two men every fifty meters, to make sure that the strands don't overlap. But saying it is one thing, and doing it is another.

"Luckily Indians take orders easily. Because you have to remember that on those catwalks it isn't like taking a stroll down Via Roma. First, they're tilted, because they have the same angle that the cable will have afterward. Second, a puff of wind is enough to make them dance, but I'll be telling you about the wind later. Third, since they have to be light and not offer any resistance to the wind, the flooring is made of wire mesh, so it's best not to look at your feet, because if you look down you see the water of the river below, mud-colored, and some little things moving in it; and from up there they might seem like little fish, but actually it's the backs of crocodiles. But I told you, in India one thing always looks like some other thing. Peraldo told me there aren't so many now, but the few that there are all come to where a bridge is being erected because they eat the garbage from the mess hall, and because they're waiting for someone to fall in. India's a fine country, but it doesn't have likable animals. Even the mosquitoes—apart from the fact that they give you malaria, and besides a topee you always have to wear a veil like ladies in olden times—they're beasts this long, and if you're not careful they give you a bite that takes away a scrap of flesh. And I was told there are also butterflies that come at night to suck your blood while you're asleep, but I never actually saw them, and as far as sleeping goes, I slept fine.

"The trick in that job of drawing wires is that the wires all have to have the same tension, and with a length like that it isn't easy. We worked two shifts, six hours each, from dawn to sunset, but then we had to organize a special team that worked at night, before the sun came up, because during the day there are always some wires exposed to the sun: they heat up and expand, while the others remain in the shade. So you have to do the calibrating before dawn, when all the wires have the same temperature. And this calibration, it was always up to me to do it.

"We went on like that for sixty days, with the idle pulley always going back and forth; and the cobweb grew, nice and taut and symmetrical; and you could already get an idea of the shape the bridge would have afterward. It was hot. I told you that; in fact, I told you I wouldn't tell you again, but it really was hot. When the sun went down it was some relief, also because I could go back to the dormitory and drink a glass and exchange a few words with Peraldo. Peraldo had started out as an unskilled laborer, then he had become a bricklayer, then a cement mixer. He had been just about everywhere, including four years in the Congo, building a dam; and he had a lot to tell, but if I start telling other people's stories besides my own there'll be no end to it.

"When the cable part of the job was finished, from the distance you could see the two cables stretching from one bank to the other with their four festoons, nice and light, just like the strands of a spiderweb. But when you looked at them close up, they were a pair of fearsome bundles, seventy centimeters thick; and we compacted them with a special machine, like a press, ring-shaped, that travels along the cable and squeezes it with a hundred-ton force. But I didn't have anything to do with this: it was an American machine; they sent it down there with its own American specialist, who snooted everybody, didn't speak to a soul, and didn't let anyone near him. Obviously he was afraid they would steal his secret.

"At this point it seemed the dirty work was done. We pulled up the vertical suspension cables in a few days, we fished them up with tackle from the pontoons down below, and it was like catching eels, but these eels weighed about a ton and a half each. And finally it was time to lay the deck; and nobody would have guessed, but this is exactly where the adventure began. I must tell you that, after the disaster of that flash flood I told you about, they didn't say a word, but they followed my advice: while I was in Calcutta they brought in an army of trucks all loaded with big rocks, and when the water subsided, they reinforced the embankments nicely. But you know about the singed cat that, afterward, was afraid of cold water: all during the rigging, from the top of my catwalk I kept an eye on the water, and I also made the engineer give me a field telephone, because I was thinking that if there was another flood, it would be best to keep ahead of it. But I never thought the danger would come from a different direction, and to judge by events, nobody was thinking of that, and the designers hadn't thought of it either.

"I never saw those designers face to face; I don't even know where they were from. But I've met others, plenty of them; and I know they come in different species. There is the elephant-designer, the kind that is always on the safe side; he doesn't care about elegance or about economy: he just doesn't want trouble, and where one would be enough, he puts four; and as a rule he's an older man, and if you think about it, you realize it's a sad thing. Then there's the stingy type, on the other hand: you'd think he had to pay for every bolt out of his own pocket. There's the parrot, who doesn't work out the plans himself but copies them, like in school, and he doesn't realize people are laughing behind his back. There's also the snail: the bureaucratic type, I mean. He moves very slowly, and the minute you touch him, he draws back and hides in his shell, which is the rule book. And, if you'll excuse the expression, I'd also call him the nitwit designer. And, finally, there's the butterfly, and I actually think the men who designed this bridge belonged to that category: they're the most dangerous type, because they are young and daring and they fool you. If you mention money and safety to them, they look at you like you were spit, and all they think about is making something new and beautiful, never considering that when a work is planned carefully it comes out beautiful automatically. Excuse me for letting myself go like this, but when a man puts his whole heart into a job, and then it ends like this bridge I'm telling you about, well, it makes you feel bad. You feel bad for lots of reasons: because you've wasted all that time, because afterward there's always a big stink with lawyers and courts and all that stuff, because even if you personally are out of it, you always feel a little responsible. But most of all, seeing a piece of work like that come down, and seeing the way it came down, one bit at a time, like it was in agony, like it was struggling, was enough to make your heart ache like when a person dies.

"And also like when a person dies, and afterward everybody says they saw it coming, from the way he was breathing, from the way he looked around, after the disaster they all had to speak their piece, even the Indian who didn't want the operation: how it was obvious, the suspensions were weak, the steel had blowholes the size of beans. The welders said the riggers didn't know their job, the crane operators said the welders didn't know theirs; and they all took it out on the engineer, and they gossiped and said he was asleep on his feet and he goofed off and he didn't know how to organize the work. And maybe they were all of them right, at least partly, or maybe none of them, because again it's sort of like with people. I've seen it lots of times: a tower, for example, checked and rechecked and tested, and it looks like it ought to stand for centuries, and it begins to teeter after a month; and another one you wouldn't give five cents for, and it never shows a crack. And if you leave it to the technical experts, the ones appointed by the court, then you're in trouble: three of them will come and they'll hand down three different opinions. I never saw an expert who was any good. Obviously, if a person dies, or a construction comes apart, there has to be a reason, but that doesn't mean there was only one, or if there was, that it's possible to discover it. But I'm getting ahead of myself.

"I told you that all during this job it was hot, every day: a damp heat it's hard to get used to; but toward the end I did get used to it. Well, when the job was finished, and the painters were already crawling up more or less everywhere, and they looked like flies on a spiderweb, I realized that all of a sudden the heat had stopped: the sun was up, but instead of the usual heat, your sweat dried on you and you felt cool. I was on the bridge, too, halfway across the first span, and besides the cool I noticed two other things that froze me in my tracks, like a hound when it points: I felt the bridge vibrating beneath my feet, and I heard something like music, but you couldn't tell what direction it was coming from: music, I mean a deep sound, distant, like when they're trying out the organ in church, because when I was a kid I used to go to church. And I realized it all came from the wind. It was the first wind I had felt since I was in India, and it wasn't a great wind, but it was steady, like the wind you feel when you drive the car slowly and hold your hand out of the window. I felt nervous— I don't know why—and I started walking toward the bank. Maybe it's an effect of our line of work: we don't like things that vibrate underfoot. I reached the abutment, I turned around, and I felt my hair stand on end, hair by hair, and all together, like each hair was waking up and wanted to run off. Because from where I was, you could see the whole length of the bridge in profile, and something was happening that you wouldn't believe. It was like, in that breath of wind, the bridge was waking up, too. Yes, like somebody who's heard a noise and wakes up, gives himself a shake, and gets ready to jump out of bed: the deck was wagging to left and right, and then it began to move vertically, too: you could see ripples running from my end to the one opposite, like when you shake a slack rope. But they weren't vibrations any more; they were waves a meter or two high, because I saw one of the painters who had dropped his things and was running toward me, and one minute I could see him, and the next, not. Like a boat at sea when the waves are high.

"Everybody ran off the bridge; even the Indians moved a

bit sharper than usual; and there was a great yelling and great confusion. Nobody knew what to do. The suspension cables had also started moving. You know how it goes in moments like that: one man says one thing, and another says something else. But after a few minutes you could see that the bridge hadn't actually stopped shaking, but the waves had become sort of stabilized. They ran and bounced from one end to the other, always with the same rhythm. I don't know who gave the order, or maybe someone just took the initiative; but I saw one of the camp tractors start over the deck of the bridge, dragging two three-inch cables. Maybe the idea was to stretch them on a diagonal, to stop the swaying. Certainly, the driver was really brave, or really irresponsible, because I don't honestly believe that those two cables, even if they had managed to anchor them, would have held together a structure like that. Imagine: the deck was eight meters wide and a meter and a half high, so just figure out how many tons that meant. Anyway, it was too late to do anything, because from that moment on, everything happened in a rush. Maybe the wind got stronger; I couldn't say, but by ten o'clock the vertical waves were four or five meters high, and you could feel the earth shaking, and hear the racket of the vertical cables loosening and tightening. The tractor driver saw things were taking a bad turn; he left the tractor on the spot and ran to the bank. And it was a good thing he did, because just afterward the deck began to twist like it was made of rubber; the tractor swerved left and right, and at a certain point it jumped the railing, or maybe smashed through it, and ended up in the river.

"One after the other, we heard what sounded like shots from a cannon. I counted: there were six of them. It was the vertical suspensions snapping: they snapped neatly, at the level of the track, and the stumps, in the backlash, flew up toward the sky. At the same time, the deck also began to bend; then it came apart and fell into the river in pieces. Some pieces, however, still hung from the girders, like rags.

"Then everything stopped. Everything was still, like after an air raid, and I don't know what I looked like, but a man next to me was all shaking and his face was greenish, though he was one of those Indians with the turban and with dark skin. In the final analysis, two spans of the deck had collapsed, almost whole, and a dozen of the vertical suspensions. On the other hand, the main cables were in place. Nothing moved. It was like a photograph, except the river kept on flowing as if nothing had happened. And yet the wind hadn't dropped; in fact, it was stronger than before. It was like somebody had wanted to do all that damage and afterward was satisfied. I had a stupid thought: I read in some book that, in ancient times, when they started building a bridge they killed a man, and they put him in the foundations; and later they killed an animal, instead, and then the bridge wouldn't fall down. But, like I said, it was a stupid thought.

"I left then. The big cables had held, after all, and so my work didn't need redoing. I learned that afterward they started arguing about the why and the wherefore, and they couldn't agree and are still arguing. As far as I'm concerned, when I saw the deck beginning to slam up and down, I immediately thought of that landing in Calcutta, and the wings of the Boeing that flapped like a bird's and gave me a nasty moment, even if I've flown lots of times. But I don't know: surely the wind had something to do with it, and I'm told they're rebuilding the bridge now, but with some vents in the deck so the wind won't meet too much resistance.

"No, I never worked on any suspension bridges after that. I left without saying goodbye to anybody, except Peraldo. It was a bad business. It was like when you're fond of a girl, and she drops you overnight, and you don't know why, and you suffer, not only because you've lost the girl, but also your self-confidence. Well, pass me the bottle and we'll have another drink. I'm paying tonight anyway. Yes, I came back to Turin, and I almost got myself into trouble with one of the girls picked out by those aunts I was telling you about at the beginning, because my morale was low and I didn't put up any resistance: but that's another story. Eventually, I got over it."

WITHOUT TIME

IT HAD RAINED all night, sometimes with silent gusts of drops so tiny they could be confused with the mist, and then in violent squalls: these would drum noisily on the corrugated metal that served as roof of the warehouse sheds built to no decipherable plan around the guest building. A humble stream that flowed nearby had swollen, and all through the night its voice penetrated my dreams, mingling with images of flood and devastation prompted by Faussone's India story. At dawn, a lazy dawn, damp and gray, we found ourselves besieged by the sacred, fertile mud of the Sarmatian plain, the dark mud, smooth and deep, that nourishes grain and engulfs invading armies.

Chickens were scratching about beneath our windows, as at home in that mud as the ducks, with whom they fought over the worms. Faussone did not fail to point out that in such conditions our chickens back home would have drowned; another confirmation of the advantages of specialization. The Russian men and women who ran the camp moved about, undaunted, in boots that came up to their knees. The two of us waited until around nine for the cars that were supposed to come and take us to our respective places of work; then we started telephoning, but by ten it was clear that the extremely polite answer "as soon as possible" meant "not today, and tomorrow only if we're lucky." The cars were stuck, broken down, assigned to other tasks; and furthermore, they had never been promised us, the soft telephone voice continued, with the familiar Russian indifference to the plausibility of an individual excuse or the reciprocal compatibility of multiple excuses. "Land without time," I remarked, and Faussone replied: "It's all a matter of not taking it to heart. Anyway, I don't know about you, but I'm paid also for this."

I was still thinking about the story he had left unresolved, about the girl his aunts had found for him, the one who nearly got him into trouble. What trouble?

Faussone was elusive. "Trouble. With a girl, three times out of four you get into trouble, especially if you don't watch out from the start. There was no understanding; all we did was contradict each other. She wouldn't let me talk and always wanted to have her say, and so then I acted the same. Mind you, she was smart, and her face was beautiful enough, but she was three years older than me and already a bit worn in the body department. I mean, she surely had her good points; but what she needed was a different man for a husband, the kind that punch the time clock and come home at the same hour and never say boo. Besides, at my age a man starts getting cranky, and for me it may even be too late."

He went to the window and he seemed pensive, in a grim mood. Outside, the rain had slacked off, but a strong wind had risen: the trees waved their boughs as if they were gesticulating, and you could see some strange, globular bundles of brush scudding along the ground, maybe a half-meter thick, or even a meter. They went by, rolling and skipping, shaped like that by evolution, to scatter seed elsewhere. Arid and at the same time obscurely alive, they seemed to be fleeing from Pier delle Vigne's forest described by Dante.

I murmured some vaguely consolatory words, the appropriate thing, and I suggested he compare his age with mine. But he resumed talking, as if he hadn't heard: "Once it was easier:

I didn't stop and think twice about it. I really was shy by nature, but at Lancia, partly for company, and partly after they put me in maintenance and I learned welding, I got bolder and gained self-confidence. Yes, welding was important, I couldn't say why. Maybe because it's not natural work, specially autogenous welding: it doesn't imitate nature, it doesn't resemble any other work; your head and your hands and your eyes have to learn each on their own, the eyes particularly, because when you put the mask over your eyes to protect you against the light, you see only black, and in the black the little glowing worm of the welding seam that advances, and it has to keep advancing at the same speed. You can't even see your hands, but if you don't do it all just right and you're even a little bit off, instead of welding you make a hole. The fact is that after I felt sure of myself as a welder, I felt sure of myself in everything, even the way I walked. And here, too, the experience I had in my father's shop came in handy, all right, because my father, rest his soul, had taught me to make copper pipes from sheeting. You couldn't buy half-finished products then: you took the sheet, you beveled the edges by hammering, you overlapped the two edges, you covered the join with borax and brass grit, and then you passed it over the coke forge, not too slow and not too fast; otherwise the brass either runs out or doesn't melt. And all without instruments. Can you get a notion of what a job it was? And then, from the big pipe you made the smaller pipes at the tube-drawing machine, pulling them with a hand windlass, and annealing again every time they went through. It's unbelievable, but in the end you could barely notice the seam, only the just-lighter line of the brass. If you ran your fingers over it, you couldn't feel a thing. Now it's all different, of course, but I have the idea that certain jobs, if they taught them in school instead of Romulus and Remus, everybody would be better off.

"I was saying: learning to weld, I learned everything, more or less. And so it happened that I got my first fairly important rigging job, and it involved welding; and I actually took a girl along with me. To tell you the truth, during the day I didn't know what to do with her; and she, too, poor thing, would follow me there and sit on the grass under the pylons, smoking one cigarette after another, getting bored; and from up top I would see her, looking tiny. The job was in the mountains, in Val d'Aosta, a beautiful spot, and it was the good season, too, the beginning of June. We had to finish rigging the pylons of a high-tension line, and then we had to draw the cables. I was twenty, I had just got my license, and when the company told me to take the pickup truck with all the equipment in it, to collect an advance and get moving, I felt proud as a king. My mother was still alive then, and she was living in the village, so I didn't tell her anything and, obviously, I told my aunts even less, because when it came to girls, they thought they had a monopoly. She was a schoolteacher and this was her vacation time. I'd known her only a month; I'd taken her dancing at Gay's. She could hardly believe it and said yes right off; she wasn't the kind of girl who makes a lot of fuss.

"You can imagine that with three things like that all at once—the girl, the important job, and the car trip—I was purring like a tuned-up engine. Being twenty years old then was the same as being seventeen today, and I drove like a fool. Though I didn't have much practice, and the pickup dragged a bit, I tried to pass everything on the road, and I would try also to give them a close shave. And remember: in those days the superhighway didn't exist yet. The girl was scared, and me—you know what it's like at that age—I got a kick out of scaring her. At a certain moment the car coughed two or three times and stopped: I raised the hood and started fiddling with the motor, giving myself all kinds of airs, though to tell you the truth I didn't understand the first thing, and I couldn't find out what the trouble was. After a while the girl got impatient. I didn't want her to, but she flagged down a Highway Patrol cop and asked him to lend us a hand. In one minute, he stuck a twig down the gas tank and showed me: there wasn't a drop of gas in it. And in fact, I knew the gauge was broken, but I'd forgotten about it because of the girl. He went off, not making any remarks; but I felt sort of cut down to size, and maybe it was a good thing, because after that I drove more reasonably and we got there without any accidents.

"We settled into a cheap little hotel, in two separate rooms, for appearances; then I reported to the offices of the power company and she went off for a stroll on her own. Compared to others I've tackled since, and I've told you about some of them, that job wasn't much; but it was the first time I was working away from the shop and I was full of enthusiasm. They led me to a pylon that was already nearly finished, they explained that the other rigger had gone sick, they gave me the blueprints and the details of the joins, and they left me there. It was a pylon of zinc-coated pipe, the Y-shaped kind. It was at an altitude of about eighteen hundred meters, and in the shadow of the rocks there was still a patch or two of snow, but the meadows were already full of flowers. You could hear water trickling and dripping all around, like after a rain, but instead, it was the thaw, because it still froze at night. The pylon was thirty meters high: the hoists were already set up, and on the ground there was the carpenters' bench, where they were preparing the pieces to be welded. They gave me a funny look, and at first I didn't understand why: then, when we got to know one another better, it turned out that the first rigger wasn't on sick leave: he was in the hospital because of an accident. To put it bluntly, he had missed his footing and fallen, luckily not from very high up, and he was in the hospital with a bunch of broken ribs. They thought it best to tell me, not that they wanted to scare me, but because they were people with common sense, old hands on the job, and seeing how I was, all full of high spirits, swaggering, with the girl down below watching me, and me clowning around, twenty meters up, without even a safety belt.

"Well, I've been on plenty of jobs by now, in Italy and abroad: sometimes they swamp you with regulations and precautions like you were retarded or an infant, specially abroad. Other times, they let you do whatever the devil you want, because anyway even if you break your skull the insurance will pay you for a new one. But in either case, if you're not careful, sooner or later you come to grief; and it's harder to learn caution than to learn the job. As a rule, you learn afterward, and it's very hard for anybody to learn until he's experienced some trouble. Luckily you experience trouble soon, and it's little things. Now there are safety inspectors, who stick their noses in everywhere, and they're right. But even if they were all geniuses and knew the secrets of every job, which isn't possible anyway because there are always new jobs and new secrets, well, do you believe there would be no more accidents? It would be like believing that if everybody obeyed the traffic laws there would be no more car crashes. But tell me if you know one driver who's never had an accident. I've thought about it lots of times: accidents shouldn't happen, but they do happen, and you have to learn to keep your eyes open all the time. Or else change jobs.

"Anyway, I got to the end of that job in one piece, and without even a bruise, and it's only because God protects drunks and lovers. But, mind you, I wasn't the one or the other: what counted for me was to look good to the girl, who was watching me from the meadow. When I think about it now I get a chill down my spine yet, and a lot of years have gone by. I went up and down the pylon, hanging from the bars, never using the ladder, as quick as Tarzan. While I did the welding, instead of sitting or straddling, the way sensible people do, I stood on my feet, or maybe even on one foot, and wham, give it the old torch. And I hardly looked at the blueprint. I really have to say that the inspector was a good man, or else he had lousy eyesight, because when I said the job was finished, he climbed up very slowly, nice and paternal, and of all my welds, and there must have been two hundred, he made me do over only about a dozen. But I could see for myself that I'd made a lot of scrawls, full of blobs and bubbles, and next to them, the welds of the man who had got hurt looked like embroidery. But that shows you how fair the world is: the careful guy had taken a fall, and me, acting the fool all the time, I hadn't gotten a scratch. And I also have to say that either my messy welding was strong or else the design was overconservative, because that pylon is still there, and it's seen a good fifteen winters at least. Well, yes, it's a weakness of mine. I won't say I suddenly get a yearning to go to India or Alaska, but when I've done a job, for better or worse, and it isn't too far off, every now and then I like to go and pay it a visit, the way you do with old relatives, and the way my father did with his stills. So if there's a holiday and I don't have anything better to do, I pick up and go. That pylon I was telling you about, well, I like going to visit it, even if it's nothing special and of all the people who go past, not one gives it a glance; but, after all, it was my first job, and I also go because of the girl I took along.

"At first, I thought she was kind of strange. I didn't have any experience, and I didn't know that all girls are strange, one way or another, and if one isn't strange that means she's really much stranger than the others, because she's abnormal; I don't know if you follow me. This one came from Calabria; I mean her parents had come up north from Calabria, but she had gone to school here in our parts, and you could only tell she came from down south because of her complexion and her hair, and because she was kind of little: from her accent you couldn't tell. To come to the mountains with me she had an argument with her family, but not all that serious, because there were seven children and one more or less didn't make much difference, and besides she was the oldest and taught school, so she was pretty independent. I told you she seemed strange to me, but mostly it was the situation that was strange, because for her, too, it was the first time she'd got away from her family and out of the city; and what's more I'd taken her to places she'd never been to, and everything amazed her, beginning with the snow in summertime and the showing off I did to impress her. Anyway, that first night up there was something I'll never forget.

"It was out of season, and in that hotel there was just the two of us, and I felt like boss of the world. We ordered a grand meal, because, well, not so much her maybe, but me, after that day in the open and all my gymnastics, I was as hungry as a stray dog; and we had plenty to drink. I can hold my wine, and you know it for that matter; but her, what with the sun she had taken, and the wine that she wasn't used to, and the fact that the two of us were alone there like in a desert, and the few people that were around we didn't know, and the thin air: the fact is that she got to laughing and talking her head off, whereas usually she was fairly reserved, and most of all she was so flushed I was worried. I think she even had a slight temperature, because if a person isn't accustomed, the sun can have that effect. In other words, to make a long story short, after supper we took a little walk outside, since there was still some light, though it was already cool, and you could see she wasn't exactly steady on her feet, or maybe she was pretending; she hung on to me and said she felt like going upstairs and sleeping. So I took her to bed, not to hers, of course, because the business of the two rooms was only for show, as if anybody up there paid attention to what we did. And I don't have to tell you about that night, because you can imagine it for yourself, and besides, on that score, if there's any need, you can ask around.

"In three days of work I had finished the welding, and since the other pylons were all ready, it was time to start drawing the cables. Seen from the ground, you know, they look like strands of yarn, but they're copper, about ten millimeters thick: not all that easy to handle, I mean. Of course, compared to that other cable job in India that I told you about, this was a lot simpler, but you have to remember it was my first job, and besides the tension has to be regulated just right, especially for the two lateral cables, the ones that hang outside the two branches of the Y; otherwise the whole base of the pylon is under stress. But don't worry: this story doesn't have any accidents, except the one that happened to the rigger who was there before me. And there weren't any accidents afterward, either; and, in fact, it's still up there and it looks like new, like I told you before. Because, you know, between a power line and a suspension bridge, like the famous one in India, there's a big difference, because people go over bridges, and on power lines only kilowatt-hours go by. I mean, power lines are a little like the books you write, which may be beautiful and all that, but, on the other hand, even if they were a bit defective, excuse the expression, nobody would die, and the only loser is the customer who bought them.

"Drawing cables, actually, isn't my line; and I should have

gone back, but after I had finished the welding, and it passed inspection, I went straight to the office and offered myself for the other job, because that way the business with the girl could last a little longer. I have to say I was bold then in a way I wouldn't dream of now: I couldn't tell you why, maybe it's only that on that occasion I needed some brass, and need creates ability. Fact is, they telephoned Turin, came to an agreement, and extended my stay. Not that I was that much smarter than anyone else, but the crew was really a bunch of numskulls, and one extra, who, all modesty aside, was fairly strong, came in handy for them. Well, would you believe it? I didn't realize, but, at least the way they did it then, it was a job for animals. Compared to that job, working at Lancia was an occupation for young ladies. Yes, copper cable is heavy, it's rigid, and at the same time it's delicate, because it's like braided, and if it scrapes against the rocks and one of the strands is damaged, then goodbye cable. It gets runs, like a woman's stocking, and you have to throw away several meters of cable and make two joins, assuming the client agrees. And whatever you do, the result is a poor job. So, to keep from scraping it over the ground, you have to hold it up, pull it taut, not let it sag, and unwind the spool from the top instead of the bottom, to gain height. In other words, our crew, which, present company excepted, was a dozen basket cases, made me think of 'The Volga Boatman,' with the difference that, instead of till death like the song says, we only heaved-ho until six in the evening. I kept my courage up thinking of the girl, but meanwhile every day that went by I got more blisters on my hands, which were a nuisance when I was with the girl; but it was an even bigger nuisance her seeing me yanking on that cable like a jackass pulling a wagon. I tried to get transferred to the hoists that lift the length of cable from the ground and attach it to the insulators, but there was nothing doing. You know how these things go: when a job is comfortable and well-paid, a mafia develops right away. Nothing doing: I had to stick with the Volga boatmen all week, and the last two days were uphill, and the cable not only wrecked my hands but skinned my shoulder, too.

"While I was laboring there, the girl wandered around the town, talking with the people; and one fine evening she told me her plan for the weekend. To tell the truth, the mere fact that she had made a plan, whatever it was, while I was hanging on to that cable, got on my nerves a bit; but out of politeness I didn't react. Or at least, I tried not to, but the girl laughed and said you could tell by the way I scratched my nose. I also had some better reasons: namely, that after six days of that job, manhandling cables, I felt more like sleeping than like climbing up mountains. Or maybe like making love, but, in any case, like being in bed. But now they had filled her mind with stuff about nature and how in a valley near the one with the power line there was a fantastic place where you could see glaciers and ibex and the mountains of Switzerland and even moraines, whatever they might be. I always thought they were some kind of edible fish. Anyway, to make a long story short, she caught on what my weak spot is, and it's pride: half joking and half serious, she called me a weakling and a slacker and some other words, in Piedmontese dialect even if she was from Calabria. And what happened was that on Saturday, the minute the camp siren blew, she pierced all the day's new blisters with a pin, dabbed the sores on my shoulder with tincture of iodine, and we packed our sacks and set off.

"Look, I don't even know why I'm telling you this story. Maybe it's because of this country, this rain that never stops, and the cars that aren't coming to pick us up: it's the contrast, in other words. I mean, because she was really right, that girl was. It really was a beautiful landscape. And also there's another contrast, when I think about it: between being twenty and being thirty-five, and between doing a thing for the first time and doing it when it's become a habit. But I'm telling these things to you, who're a lot older than me, and I have an idea there's no need.

"She had asked around, like I said, and had decided that for our honeymoon (that was the word she used, but I wasn't all that convinced) we should go to a little hut for climbers; I don't remember the name now, but the place would be hard for me to forget, and the night we spent there. Not because we made love, but because of the rest of it. Now I've been told they lower them there with helicopters, but in those days these huts were pretty crude, and most people, even those bums who sleep in the Porta Nuova station, if you forced them to sleep there, they'd complain. It was like a half-barrel, of tin plate, two meters by two, with a little door to get in, like a cat door, and inside only a horsehair mattress, a few blankets, a little stove the size of a shoebox, and if you were lucky, some hard tack left behind by the last ones there. Since it was in the form of a half-cylinder, the hut was maybe a meter high, more or less, and to get inside you had to crawl on hands and knees. On the roof there were some heavy copper strips, which acted as lightning rods but also as braces against the wind, so a storm wouldn't blow everything away; and also, sticking straight up, there was a shovel with a handle more than two meters high, so it would stick out of the snow in the between-seasons and act as a signal. You could also use it for shoveling snow when the hut was buried.

"Water wasn't a problem. That hut was set on a spur of rock two meters above a flat glacier. I was dying to take a walk on it, but the girl said it was dangerous, because of the crevasses. And if you ended up in a crevasse they didn't even come to pull you out, because they knew in advance it was your fault, and besides, it wasn't worth the trouble because generally by the time you hit bottom you're already dead from the bashing and the terror, and if you're not dead, you die of the cold before the rescue team can arrive. They had explained all this to her down in the valley, at the guides' office. Whether or not it's all true, I couldn't guarantee, because seeing a pair of greenhorns like us, they maybe wanted to take their own precautions. I was saying water wasn't a problem, because for several weeks the weather had been hot, the snow of the glacier was melting, the ice remained bare, and in the ice the water had dug like little greenish channels, a lot of them, all parallel, like hatching. You see, to discover strange things sometimes you don't have to go to Alaska. And the water that ran in them had a taste I'd never tasted before, and I couldn't explain it to you, because you know how hard it is to explain tastes and smells, except with examples, like if you say the smell of garlic or the taste of salami. But I would actually say that water tasted like sky, and, in fact, it came straight down from the sky.

"Eating wasn't a problem, either, because we had brought everything we needed with us, and we had gathered some wood along the way and we even made a fire and cooked over it, like they used to do. And when night came, we realized that over our heads we had a sky like I had never seen or even dreamed of, so full of stars that it actually seemed overloaded to me; I mean that for two people like us, from the city, a rigger and a schoolteacher, it was an exaggeration, a wasted luxury. I guess we're all crazy when we're twenty! Imagine: we spent about half the night wondering why there are so many stars, what's the use of them, how long they've been there, and also what's the use of us, and what happens after we die: I mean questions that for anybody with a head on his shoulders have no meaning, specially for a rigger. And the second half of the night we spent the way you can imagine, but in such complete silence and such deep darkness that we seemed to be in another world and we were almost afraid, also because every now and then we heard sounds we didn't understand, like distant thunder or like a wall crumbling, distant, but profound, that made the rock shake beneath our backs.

"But then, at a certain point in the night, we began to hear a different sound, and this one really did scare me, and no almost about it: real fear, and I actually put on my shoes and started to go outside to see what it was, but so reluctantly that when the girl said in a whisper: 'No, no, skip it, you'll take cold,' I immediately shifted into reverse and got back under the blanket. It sounded like a saw, but a saw with snaggleteeth, dulled, trying to saw at the metal of the hut; and the hut was like a sound box that produced an unbelievable racket. It scraped wearily, one or two blows, and then silence, and then again a blow or two. Between scrapes you could hear some puffing and a few coughs. Well, the moral of the story is that with the excuse that it was cold, we stayed in there until we could see a little line of light around the door, also because that sawing sound had stopped; there was only the puffing, and it was getting fainter and fainter. I went outside, and there was an ibex, sprawled against the side of the hut. It was big, but it looked sick, ugly, its fur all patchy; it was drooling and coughing. Maybe it was about to die, and we were sad to think it had tried to wake us to ask for help, or else it wanted to come and die near us.

"Would you believe it? It was like a signal, as if by scraping its horns against the metal it wanted to tell us something. With that girl I had thought it was a beginning; and, instead, it was the end. That whole day we didn't know what to say to each other; and then, after we were back in Turin, I would telephone her and suggest things, and she wouldn't say no, but when she accepted, it was with a forget-it tone that was easy to understand. I don't know; she must've found somebody better than me, one of those guys who punch their card, and I'm not saying she wasn't right, considering the life I lead. Now, for instance, she'd be alone."

THE DOOR was flung open, and along with a gust of air redolent of mushrooms, a driver entered, bundled into a rainproof overall, glistening with rain. He looked like a deep-sea diver. He explained to us that the car had come and was outside, waiting for us, at the gate. Two cars? No, not two. One, but very big. We explained to him that we had to go in two different directions, but he said that didn't matter: he would accompany first me and then him, or vice versa, as we chose. Outside, at the gate, we found not a car but a tourist bus, with fifty seats, all for us. We would arrive at our respective places, Faussone two hours late, and I, at least three. "Land without time," Faussone repeated.

THE BEVEL GEAR

BECAUSE YOU MUSTN'T think that our country is the only place where they play certain tricks, and that only our people are good at shortchanging and we never get taken in ourselves. Besides, I don't know how much you've traveled, but I've traveled a lot, and I've discovered that you shouldn't think countries are the way they teach you in school and the way they are in jokes. You know what I mean: all the English are sedate and proper; the French, *blagueurs;* the Germans, hardheaded; and the Swiss, honest. Ha! it's not like that, not at all. It's the same the whole world over."

In the space of a few days, winter had hit us: outside a dry, hard snow was falling; every now and then a gust of wind would fling a handful of tiny grains of hail against the windows of the mess. Through the swirling snow you could glimpse, all around, the black siege of the forest. Without success, I tried to interrupt Faussone and protest my innocence: I haven't traveled as much as he has, but surely enough to realize the futility of the clichés that are the basis of popular geography. Nothing doing: arresting one of Faussone's sto-

ries is like arresting a tidal wave. At this point he was in full
spate, and it was not hard to discern, beyond the drapery of
the prologue, the corpulence of the story that was beginning
to take shape. We had finished our coffee, which was loath-
some, as in all countries (Faussone had told me this) where the
accent on the word for coffee falls on the first syllable; and I
had offered him a cigarette, forgetting he doesn't smoke, and
that I myself, the night before, had become aware that I was
smoking too much and had then made a solemn vow to give it
up. But, honestly, what can you do after coffee like that, and
on an evening like that?

"It's the same the whole world over, like I was saying. Take
this country here, too, because this is the very country where
the story happened. No, not now: it was six or seven years
ago. You remember that boat trip, with Difference, that wine,
and that lake that was almost a sea, and the dam I pointed to
in the distance? We'll have to go there one Sunday; I'd like to
show it to you, because it's a fine piece of work. These people
are kind of slow-witted, but for the big jobs they're better
than us, no two ways about it. Well, the biggest crane on the
site—I was the one who rigged it. I mean, I'm the one who organized the job, because it's one of those machines that erect
themselves. They come straight up from the earth, like mushrooms do, and it's a pretty sight to see. You have to forgive me
if I talk about it every now and then, this business of rigging
cranes; by now you know I'm one of those men who like their
jobs. Even if it's uncomfortable sometimes: that time, for example, we did the job in January, working Sundays, and everything froze, even the grease for the cables, and we had to
soften it with steam. At a certain point, ice formed on the
frame, often an inch thick and hard as iron, and we couldn't
fit the pieces together. I mean they would slide all right, but
by the time they got to the top, they were stuck.

"Still, one way or another, we reached the day of the final
inspection. Some ways were worse than another, like I mentioned to you; but on the job, and not only on the job, if there
aren't troubles, it's no fun telling about it afterward. And, you
know, you said so yourself: telling about things is one of the
joys of life. I wasn't born yesterday, and obviously I had al-

ready checked the job all out on my own, piece by piece: all the movements went beautifully, also the loading test. No bones about it. Inspection day is always like a celebration: I gave myself a nice clean shave, put some brilliantine on my hair (well, yes, here in the back, where I still have some). I slipped on my corduroy jacket, and there I was on the site, all ready and waiting, a good half-hour ahead of time.

"The interpreter arrives, the chief engineer arrives, and also one of those little old women of theirs that you never know what they're for, they stick their noses everywhere, they ask a lot of meaningless questions, they write your name on a piece of paper, look at you suspiciously, and then they sit down in a corner and start knitting. The engineer of the dam also arrives, and it's a lady engineer: nice, sweet as pie, with a great pair of shoulders on her, and a broken nose like a boxer. We had run into each other various times in the mess and had even struck up a kind of friendship: she had a good-for-nothing husband, three children whose pictures she showed me; and before she got her university degree, she had driven a tractor in a *kolkhoz*. At table she was a sight to see; she ate like a lion, and before the meal she would toss off a hundred grams of vodka like nothing at all: the kind of person I like. Some loafers arrived, but I didn't know who they were, that early in the morning they were already half drunk. One had a big bottle of liquor, and they went on drinking by themselves.

"Finally the inspector arrived. He was a dark little man, in a dark suit, maybe forty, with one shoulder higher than the other, and a face like his digestion was bad. He didn't even look Russian: he looked like a starving cat, yes, one of those cats that get the habit of eating lizards, then they don't grow, and turn sad; they don't lick their fur any more, and instead of meowing they go *hhhhh*. But inspectors are almost all like that: it's not a jolly profession. If you don't have some kind of mean streak you aren't a good inspector, and if you happen not to have the mean streak at first, you develop it as time goes by, because everybody glares at you, and life isn't easy. Still, they're necessary; I understand that myself, like laxatives are necessary.

"When he arrives, everybody shuts up. He switches on the

current, climbs the ladder, and closes himself in the cabin, because in those days cranes had all their controls in the cabin. Now? Now they're on the ground, because of lightning. He closes himself in the cabin, yells down to make room, and everybody steps out of the way. He tests the transmission, and everything goes fine. He shifts the dolly on the arm: it moves as smooth as a boat on a lake. He has a ton-weight attached and he pulls it up: perfect, like the machinery didn't feel the weight at all. Then he tests the rotation, and all hell breaks loose: the arm, a fine arm more than thirty meters long, turns in jerks, with a creaking that would wring your heart. You know, when you hear equipment that isn't working right, that jerks and grinds, it hurts you like it was a human being. It makes two or three jolts, then stops abruptly, and the whole structure shudders and sways from right to left, and left to right, like it was saying no, for God's sake stop this.

"I started to rush up the ladder, and meanwhile I was yelling to the guy up there for the love of God not to move, not to try any other operations. I get to the top, and I swear it was like being in a storm at sea; and there's my little man, nice and calm, sitting on the seat, writing his report in his notebook. At that time I didn't know much Russian, and he didn't know any Italian at all: we got along with a smattering of English; but you can imagine, what with the cabin still swaying, the fright, and the language barrier, our whole argument was crazy. He kept saying *nyet nyet*, that the machine was kaputt, and he wasn't going to pass it. I was trying to explain to him that before the report was signed, I wanted to figure everything out calmly. I already had my suspicions: first, because, like I told you, I had run my own tests the day before and everything had gone fine; second, because I had realized some time ago that there were certain Frenchmen hanging around, and there was a bid open for three more cranes like this one, and I knew that for this crane our company had won by a hair, and the French had come in second.

"It's not for the boss's sake, you understand. I don't give that much of a damn about the boss, so long as he pays me what's right and lets me do the jobs my way. No, it's for the work itself: setting up a machine like that, working on it with your hands and your head for days and days, seeing it grow like that, tall and straight, strong and slim as a tree; and then if it doesn't work, you suffer. It's like a pregnant woman whose baby comes out crippled or retarded; I don't know if you follow me."

I followed him. As I was listening to Faussone, inside me a hypothesis was slowly coagulating, something I didn't then develop further, but I'll submit it to the reader now: the noun "freedom" notoriously has many meanings, but perhaps the most accessible form of freedom, the most subjectively enjoyed, and the most useful to human society consists of being good at your job and therefore taking pleasure in doing it.

"Anyway, I waited for him to come down, and then I started taking a good look at the situation. There was surely something wrong with the bevel gear . . . what's there to laugh about?"

I wasn't laughing; I was only smiling, without realizing it. I hadn't had any dealings with bevel gears since I was thirteen, when I stopped playing with my Meccano set, and the memory of that worklike game, lonely and intense, and of that minuscule bevel gear of shiny, milled brass, had touched me for a moment.

"That's a very delicate part, you know, much more than conventional gears. Even more difficult to rig, and if you use the wrong kind of grease, they seize up something great. For that matter, I don't know, it's never happened to me, but to do a job without some trouble, a job where everything runs smoothly, must be pretty boring; and in the long run it makes you stupid. I believe men are made like cats, and excuse me if I bring up cats again, but it's because of the profession. If they don't know what to do, if they don't have mice to catch, they scratch one another, they run off across the roofs, or else they climb trees and maybe howl then because they don't know how to get down. I really believe that to live happily you have to have something to do, but it shouldn't be too easy, or else something to wish for, but not just any old wish: something there's a hope of achieving.

"But to get back to the bevel gear. In five minutes I'd caught on: the alignment. You understand? The most vulnerable spot, because the bevel gear is what you might call the heart of a crane, and the alignment is. . . . Well, without alignment the gear is ready for the junk heap after two revolutions. I won't go into details: somebody had been there, somebody in the business, and had redrilled one by one all the holes of the support and had remounted the base of the gear, which looked straight but was actually out of line. It was the work of an artist, and if it hadn't been for the fact that they wanted to screw me, I would even have paid them compliments; but instead I was mad as a bull. Obviously, it had been those Frenchmen, either with their own hands or with somebody else's help; I don't know, maybe with the inspector, the one who was in such a hurry to write his report.

". . . Sure, of course, we lodged a protest: witnesses, another inspection, lawsuit. But it still sticks there, like a shadow, like a grease stain, and it's hard to get it off. Years have passed, but the lawsuit is still going on: eighty pages of testimony by experts from the Technological Institute of Sverdlovsk, with load test reports, photographs, X rays, everything. How do you think it will end? I already know what happens when things of iron become things of paper. It ends wrong."

ANCHOVIES I

I RAISED MY MOUTH from the dish, repeating to myself the words from Dante, "you wish me to renew. . . ." Faussone's conclusion had touched a raw nerve. That very same Technological Institute of Sverdlovsk was my adversary at the moment; it had torn me from my factory, my laboratory, from my loved-hated desk and had relegated me to this place. Like Faussone, I also lived in the menacing shadow of a bilingual dossier; I, too, had landed here in the role of defendant. I even had the impression that this episode was somehow a turning point, a singular moment in my earthly itinerary; and for that matter, my strange destiny had decreed that the turning points in my life should occur in this great, strange country.

Since the defendant's role is uncomfortable, this was to be my last adventure as a chemist. Afterward: full stop, paragraph. With nostalgia, but without misgivings, I would choose another road, since I had that option and still felt strong enough: the road of the teller of stories. My own stories as long as any remained in my sack, then other people's stories, stolen, robbed, extorted, or received as gifts: his, for example, but also stories of everyone and no one, stories from the air, painted on gauze, so long as they had a meaning for me or could give the reader a moment of wonder or laughter. Somebody once said life begins at forty: well, for me, it would begin, or rebegin, at fifty-five. For that matter, it was possible that, having spent more than thirty years sewing together long molecules presumably useful to my neighbor and performing the parallel task of convincing my neighbor that my molecules really were useful to him, I might have learned something about sewing together words and ideas, or about the general and specific properties of my colleague, man.

After some hesitation, and at my repeated request, Faussone declared I was free to tell his stories, and that's how this book was born. As for the investigation of the court-appointed experts in Sverdlovsk, he regarded me with cautious curiosity: "So you're here because of a foul-up. Don't take it to heart. I mean, don't take it too much to heart; otherwise you're done for. It happens in the best of families, making a mistake or having to patch up somebody else's mistake; and anyway, a profession without screw-ups is something I can't imagine. Well, I mean, they do exist, but they're not real professions; they're like cows out to pasture, but at least they give milk, and besides they get slaughtered. Or like those old men playing bowls in the square, talking to themselves. Tell me about it, this screw-up of yours. It's your turn this time, since I've already told you a lot of mine. Then I can make a comparison. And besides, hearing other people's troubles, you forget your own."

I told him.

"My profession, my real one, the profession I studied in school and that has kept me alive so far is the profession of chemist. I don't know if you have a clear idea of it, but it's a bit like yours; only we rig and dismantle very tiny constructions. We're divided into two main branches, those who rig and those who dismantle or break down, and both kinds are like blind people with sensitive fingers. I say blind because, actually, the things we handle are too small to be seen, even with the most powerful microscopes: so we've invented various intelligent gadgets to recognize them without seeing them. Here you have to bear in mind one thing: for example, a blind man has no trouble telling you how many bricks there are on a table, what position they're in, how far apart; but if instead of bricks there were grains of rice or, worse still, marbles, the blind man, as you can imagine, would have trouble saying where they are, because the minute you touch them they move. Well, that's our situation. And lots of times, moreover, we have the impression not only of being blind, but of being blind elephants at a watch-mender's desk, because our fingers are too crude to handle those tiny things that we have to attach or detach.

"Those who dismantle, the analytical chemists, in other words, have to be able to take a structure apart piece by piece without damaging it, or at least without damaging it too much; then they have to line up the pieces on the desk, naturally without ever seeing them, but recognizing them one by one. Then they say in what order the pieces were attached. Nowadays they have wonderful instruments that abbreviate the process, but in the old days it was all done by hand, and it took unbelievable patience.

"But I've always been a rigger-chemist, one of those who make syntheses, who build structures to order, in other words. They give me a model, say, something like—"

Here, as Faussone had done time and again to explain his structures, I also picked up a paper napkin and scrawled a drawing, more or less like this:

$$
\begin{array}{c}
\text{H} \\
\text{N—CO} \\
\text{CH}_2 \quad \text{N—} \\
\text{CH}_2\text{—NHCO—N—CH}_2
\end{array}
$$

$$
\begin{array}{l}
\text{CO—N—} \\
\text{—N} \qquad \text{CH}_2 \\
\text{CH}_2\text{—N} \\
\quad \text{CO—NHCH}_2\text{—N} \qquad \text{CO—N} \\
\qquad\qquad\qquad \text{CH}_2 \qquad \text{CH}_3 \\
\qquad\qquad\qquad \text{CH}_2\text{—N} \\
\qquad\qquad\qquad\quad \text{CO—NHCH}_2\text{—N} \qquad \text{CO—N—} \\
\qquad\qquad\qquad\qquad\qquad\qquad \text{CH}_2 \qquad \text{CH}_2 \\
\qquad\qquad\qquad\qquad\qquad\qquad \text{CH}_2\text{—N} \\
\qquad\qquad\qquad\qquad\qquad\qquad\quad \text{CO—NH—CH}_2\text{—}
\end{array}
$$

". . . or else, sometimes I make it myself, and then I have to manage somehow. With a bit of experience, it's easy to tell right away the structures that can work from those that will be unstable or immediately go to pieces, and also from the other kind that are possible only on paper. But we are still blind, even in the best circumstances, that is, with structures that are simple and stable. Blind, and we don't have those tweezers we often dream of at night, the way a thirsty man dreams of springs, that would allow us to pick up a segment, hold it firm and straight, and paste it in the right direction on the segment that has already been assembled. If we had those tweezers (and it's possible that, one day, we will), we would have managed to create some lovely things that so far only the Almighty has made, for example, to assemble—perhaps not a frog or a dragonfly—but at least a microbe or the spore of a mold.

"But for the present we don't have those tweezers, and when you come right down to it, we're bad riggers. We really are like elephants who have been given a closed box containing all the pieces of a watch: we are very strong and patient, and we shake the box in every direction and with all our strength. Maybe we even warm it up, because heating is another form of shaking. Well, sometimes, if the watch isn't too complicated, if we keep on shaking, we succeed in getting it together; but, as you can imagine, it's more reasonable to proceed a bit at a time, first attaching two pieces, then adding a third, and so on. It takes more patience, but actually you get there first. And most of the time that's the way we do it.

"As you can see, you people are luckier, because you can watch your structures grow beneath your hands and before your eyes, and you can check them progressively as they come up, and if you make a mistake, it's easy to correct it. True, we have one advantage: a rigging job of ours doesn't produce just a single structure, but a whole lot of them at once. A lot, a number you can't even conceive, a number with twenty-five or twenty-six digits. If this weren't the case, obviously—"

"Obviously, you could change professions," Faussone said, completing the sentence. "Go on. A man learns something every day."

"We could change professions. And, in fact, sometimes we do: for example, when things go wrong, and our infinitesimal structures don't work out, or maybe they all do work out, but with a detail that the model didn't anticipate, and we don't realize it immediately, because we're blind. The client realizes it first. Yes, that's the very reason I'm here now: not to write stories. The stories, if anything, are a by-product, at least for the present. I'm here with a letter in my pocket, a complaint because the product supplied supposedly didn't meet specifications. If our side is right, all well and good, and they even pay for my trip; but if their side is right, there's six hundred tons of goods we have to replace, plus damages, because it will be our fault if a certain factory doesn't achieve the quota established by the Plan.

"I'm a rigger-chemist; I told you that, but I didn't tell you that my specialty is paint. It's not a specialty I chose myself, for any personal reason; it's just that after the war I needed a job, urgently, and I found one in a paint factory, and I thought, Better than nothing. And then I didn't dislike the job, so I ended up becoming a specialist, and I stayed on. I soon realized that manufacturing paints is a strange profession. Practically speaking, it means making films, artificial skins. In fact, paints have to have many of the qualities of our natural skin, and, mind you, that's no trifle, because skin is a valuable product. Our chemical skins, too, have to have qualities that contradict one another: they have to be flexible and at the same time resist wounds; they have to stick to the flesh, the substrate, that is, but dirt mustn't stick to them; they have to have nice delicate colors, and at the same time withstand light. They have to be permeable to water and also be waterproof, and that is so contradictory that even our human skin is unsatisfactory, in the sense that it actually does resist rain and seawater fairly well. I mean it doesn't shrink or expand or dissolve, but if you go too far, rheumatism develops; it's a sign that a little water does get through, and sweat absolutely has to get through, but only from inside toward outside. I told you: it's not simple.

"They had given me the job of devising an enamel to coat

the inside of tin cans for food, for exportation (the enamel, that is, not the cans) to this country. As a skin, it could have been a splendid skin, I swear: it had to adhere to the tin plate, resist sterilization at 120 degrees centigrade, bend around a given mandrel without cracking, resist abrasion when tested with a gadget I won't try to describe to you. But, above all, it had to withstand a whole series of assaults, by things not normally seen in our laboratories: I mean, anchovies, vinegar, lemon juice, tomato (the enamel was not to absorb the red coloring), brine, olive oil, and so on. It wasn't to take on the odor of these things or impart any odor to them: but to test these characteristics we had to rely just on the inspector's nose. Finally, the enamel had to be capable of application with certain nonstop machines, where the sheet of metal enters on one side, unrolling from the spool; receives the enamel from a kind of inking roll; passes into the baking oven; and is wound on the shipping roll. In these conditions, it should produce a smooth and shiny coating, a golden-yellow color, whose shade had to lie between two color samples attached to the specification. You follow me?"

"Of course," Faussone answered, in an almost offended tone. But perhaps the reader isn't following me, here and elsewhere, when it's a question of mandrels, molecules, ball bearings, and lugs. Well, I'm sorry and I apologize, but in some cases there are no synonyms. If, as is likely, in his youth the reader accepted the seafaring tales of the nineteenth century, then he digested bowsprits and fo'c'sles; so he must be brave, use his imagination, or consult a dictionary. It may be useful for him anyway, since we live in a world of molecules and ball bearings.

"I must tell you at once that I wasn't being asked to invent anything—similar enamels already exist—but I had to pay attention to details, to make sure the product would pass all the tests, especially the baking time, which had to be fairly short. Essentially, it was a question of devising a kind of sticking plaster based on a fabric of average compactness, with the weave not too tight, so it would retain some elasticity, but not too loose either; otherwise the anchovies and the tomatoes could get past it. It also had to have a lot of stout little hooks, to shrink to a sort of felt and to stick to the substrate during baking; but it should lose them after that same baking, because otherwise it might pick up color or odor or taste. Naturally it could contain no toxic substances. You see, this is how we chemists think: we try to imitate you, like that ape helper of yours. In our mind, we construct a little mechanical model, though we know it's crude and childish, and we follow it as far as we can, but always with a nagging envy of you men with five senses, who fight between sky and earth against old enemies and work in centimeters and meters instead of dealing with our invisible, tiny sausages and nets. Our way of getting tired is different from yours. It doesn't lie along the spine, but higher up; it doesn't come at the end of a wearisome day, but when you've been trying to make sense of something and have failed. As a rule, sleep doesn't cure it. Yes, I feel that way to-night; that's what makes me talk about it.

"So everything was going well: we sent the sample to the State Industry Board, we waited seven months, and the answer was positive. We sent a sample drum of enamel here to the plant, we waited another nine months, and the letter of acceptance came, along with the type approval and an order for three hundred tons. Immediately afterward, God knows why, there was another order, with a different signature, for another three hundred, marked Most Urgent this time. Probably it was a duplicate of the first order, sent through some bureaucratic mix-up; in any case, it was official, and it was just what was needed to put our annual turnover in good shape. We had all become very polite, and around the plant all you could see was big smiles: six hundred tons of an enamel fairly easy to produce, all the same type, and at a price that wasn't bad.

"We're conscientious people. From every batch we religiously took a sample and tested it in the lab, to make sure the samples still met all the requirements I told you about. Our lab was full of new and pleasant smells, and the testing bench was like a grocery. All was well, we felt we were in a foolproof situation, and every Friday, when the fleet of trucks set out, taking the drums to Genoa to be loaded on the ships, we held a little celebration, using some of the provisions supplied for the tests, 'rather than let them go to waste.'

"Then the first alarm signal came: a polite telex requesting us to repeat the test with anchovies on a certain batch that had already been shipped. The girl who performed the tests laughed and said she'd repeat the test immediately, but she was quite sure of her results: that stuff would be proof even against sharks. But I knew how these things went, and I began to feel some cramps in my stomach."

Faussone's face crinkled in an unexpected, sad smile. "That's right. I get a pain here, on my right side: I think it's my liver. But for me a man who's never had a negative test isn't a man; it's like he was still at his first communion. Say what you like, I know this kind of thing; at first they make you feel awful, but if you don't go through it, you never grow up. It's like flunking in school."

"I knew how these things went. After two days had passed, another telex came. And this one wasn't polite at all. That batch didn't stand up to anchovies, and neither did the later batches that had arrived in the meanwhile. We were to send at once, by air, a thousand kilograms of guaranteed enamel, otherwise—frozen payment and a lawsuit for damages. Now the temperature began to rise, and the lab filled up with anchovies: Italian, large and small, Spanish, Portuguese, Norwegian; and we deliberately let two hectograms spoil, to see what effect they had on the coated tin. As you can imagine, we were all fairly smart in the field of paints, but none of us was an anchovies expert. We prepared one test piece after another, like lunatics, hundreds of them a day. We would put them in contact with anchovies from every sea in the world, but nothing happened. In our lab, all went well. Then it occurred to us that perhaps Soviet anchovies were more aggressive than ours. We immediately sent a telex, and a week later the specimen was on our table. They had done things in grand style: a thirty-kilo can, where thirty grams would have been enough. Maybe it was a special size for boarding schools or for the armed forces. And I must say they were delicious, because we also tasted them. But nothing doing. They, too, had no effect whatsoever on any of the test strips, not even on the ones that had been badly prepared, on purpose, to reproduce the most unfavorable conditions: underbaked, belowstandard thickness, bent before the test.

"Meanwhile the report from Sverdlovsk had arrived: I mentioned it before. I have it upstairs in my room, in the desk drawer, and I swear, to me it seems to stink. No, not of anchovies: it seems to give off a stink from the drawer, poisoning the air, especially at night, because at night I have strange dreams. Maybe it's my fault; I'm taking it too much to heart. . . ."

Faussone looked sympathetic. He interrupted me to order a couple of vodkas from the girl dozing behind the counter: he explained that this vodka was special, illegally distilled, and in fact it had an unusual odor, pleasant, which I preferred not to inquire about.

"Drink. It'll do you good. Of course, you take it to heart. Only natural. When a man puts his signature on something, whether it's a promissory note or a crane or an anchovy—sorry, I meant to say a paint—he's responsible for it. Drink. That way, you'll sleep well tonight and you won't dream of tests, and tomorrow morning you'll wake up without a headache. Wait and see. This is black-market stuff, but it's genuine. Now tell me how it ended."

"It hasn't ended, and I don't even feel up to saying how or when it might end. I've been here for twelve days, and I don't know how long I'll stay; every morning they send for me, sometimes a limousine, sometimes an army vehicle; they take me to the lab, and then nothing happens. The interpreter comes and apologizes: either the technician is absent, or there's a power failure, or the whole staff has been called to a meeting. It's not that they're rude to me, but they seem to forget I'm here. So far I haven't spoken with the technician for more than half an hour; he showed me their test strips, I'm racking my brain, but they're nothing at all like ours. Ours are smooth and clean; these have all sorts of little lumps. Obviously, something happened during shipment, but I can't imagine what. Or else there's something wrong with their tests, but, as you well know, putting the blame on someone else, especially the client, is bad policy. I told the technician I wanted to observe the whole cycle, the preparation of the samples, from the beginning to the end. He seemed cross at the idea, but he said all right; then he hasn't shown up since. Instead of the technician, I have to talk with a terrible woman. Madam Kondratova is small, fat, elderly, with a haggard face; and there's no way of making her stick to the subject. Instead of talking about paint, she spends the whole time telling me the story of her life, a horrible story: she was in Leningrad during the siege, her husband and her two sons died at the front, and she was working in an arms factory, at a lathe, and the temperature was ten below zero. I feel very sorry for her, but she makes me mad, too, because in four days my visa expires, and how can I go back to Italy without having settled anything, and especially without having figured anything out?"

"Did you tell this woman your visa's about to expire?"

"No, I don't think she has any connection with my visa."

"Listen to me: tell her. From your description, my guess is that she's fairly important, and when a visa expires, these people get on it right away, because otherwise they're in the soup themselves. Try it. No harm in trying. You're not risking anything."

He was right. At the mere mention of the imminent expiration of my visa, a surprising change took place around me, like the finale of a silent movie. All of them, Kondratova in the lead, brusquely accelerated their movements and their words; they became suddenly understanding and helpful; the lab opened its doors to me; and the man who prepared the strips announced that he was entirely at my disposal.

I didn't have much time left, and first of all I asked to examine the contents of the latest drums. It wasn't easy to identify them, but in half a day I succeeded. We prepared the samples with all due care: they came out smooth and glossy, and after a conjugal night with the anchovies their appearance was unchanged. We had to conclude that either the enamel altered under local storage conditions or else something happened in the course of the sampling made by the Russians. On the morning of my departure I just had time to test one of the oldest drums: some suspect samples resulted, streaked and gritty, but at that point there was no time to investigate further. My request for an extension had been rejected. Faussone came to say goodbye at the station, and we parted, exchanging promises to get together, either there or in Turin, but most likely there. In fact, he had several months' work still ahead of him: with a crew of Russian riggers, he was perfecting one of their colossal excavators, tall as a three-story house, which can move over any terrain, proceeding on four enormous paws like prehistoric saurians; and I had to settle two or three things back at the factory, but I would unquestionably return within a month at most. Kondratova had told me that one way or another they could manage for a month: that very day she had received word that in another factory they were using a German enamel that apparently caused no trouble. While they were trying to clear up our difficulty, they would send urgently for some of that enamel. Still, with an absence of logic that surprised me, she insisted I come back as soon as possible: "all things considered," our enamel was preferable. For her part, she would do everything she could to have me issued another, renewable visa.

Faussone asked me, since I was going to Turin, if I would deliver a package to his aunts, a letter, and his excuses: he would be spending All Saints' on the job. The package was light but bulky; the letter was only a note, with the address written in the clear, meticulous, and slightly affected hand of someone who has studied mechanical drawing. He told me to be careful not to lose the document declaring the value of the package, and we parted.

THE AUNTS

FAUSSONE'S AUNTS lived in an old apartment on Via Lagrange, a little two-story building cramped between more recent (but equally run-down) constructions, at least three times as high. The facade was humble, an undefined earthen color, against which some now barely discernible fake windows and fake balconies had been painted a brick red. Stairway B, the one I was looking for, stood at the back of the courtyard. I paused to observe the yard, as two housewives watched me suspiciously from their respective landings. The yard and the entrance portico were paved in gravel, and under the portico were two parallel strips for vehicles, granite slabs furrowed and worn by the passage of generations of wagons. In one corner there was a laundry trough, long in disuse: it had been filled with earth, and a weeping willow was growing in it. In another corner there was a pile of sand, obviously dumped there for some repair job and then forgotten. Rain had eroded it into shapes that suggested the Dolomites, and cats had dug some comfortable nests in it. Opposite was the wooden door of an ancient latrine, the lower part rotten from humidity and alkaline fumes, the upper part still covered by a gray paint that had cracked over the darker base, giving it the look of a crocodile's hide. The two landings ran around three sides, divided only by rusty gates with iron spikes that jutted out beyond the railings. Eight meters from the pretentious, traffic-jammed street, in that yard you breathed a vaguely cloistered air, along with the unassuming charm of things once useful and now long abandoned.

On the third floor I found the brass plate I was looking for: Oddenino Gallo. Sisters of his mother, then, not of his father: or perhaps distant aunts, in the vague sense of the word. Both of them came to the door, and at first glance I seemed to notice between them that curious resemblance that often, absurdly, we remark between two people, however different, whom we happen to meet under the same circumstances and at the same time. No, they didn't really look much alike: nothing beyond an undefinable family air, a solid bone structure, the meek propriety of their dress. One aunt had white hair; the other, dark brown. Dyed? No, not dyed. Seen closer, it revealed a few white strands at the temples, a guarantee. They took the package, thanked me, and made me sit on a little two-seated sofa, rather worn, of a shape I had never seen before: almost halved by a narrow neck and with the two seats at a right angle. The brown-haired sister sat on the other half, the white-haired one on a small armchair facing us.

"Will you excuse me if I open the letter? Tino writes us so little, you know . . . yes, here's all he says: 'Dearest aunts, I am taking advantage of a friend's kindness to send you this present. Affectionate greetings, a hug and kiss from your Tino, as ever.' And that's that. He won't suffer from eyestrain, that's for sure. So you're a friend of his?"

I explained that I wasn't exactly a friend, what with the age difference, for one thing, but we ran into each other in those distant parts, we spent so many evenings together. In other words, we had been good company for each other, and he had told me many interesting things. I caught the white-haired aunt exchanging a rapid look with her sister. "Really?" the latter asked. "With us, he hardly speaks, you see. . . ."

I tried to repair the damage: in such places there wasn't much entertainment, none, in fact, and being two Italians in the midst of all those foreigners, it became natural to talk. For that matter, he told me only about his work as a rule. Minding my manners, I tried to address first one, then the other aunt equally; but I had a hard time. The white-haired aunt rarely turned her gaze on me; mostly she looked at the floor, or else, if I addressed her directly, she would keep her eyes glued on her dark sister's. The few times she said anything, it was to her sister, as if she spoke a language I couldn't understand and the dark sister had to act as interpreter. When it was the dark one who spoke, however, the white one would still stare at her, leaning slightly forward in her seat, as if to keep watch, ready to catch her out in any mistake.

The dark sister was talkative and good-humored: I quickly learned a great deal about her: that she was a widow, childless; that she was sixty-three and her sister sixty-six; that her name was Teresa, and the white-haired one was Mentina, which was short for Clementina; that her late husband had been a mechanic in the merchant marine, but then with the war they had assigned him to a destroyer, and then he was declared missing in the Adriatic at the beginning of 1943, the very year Tino was born. They had just married. Mentina, on the other hand, had never married.

". . . but tell me about Tino. He's well, isn't he? He isn't catching cold, up on those scaffoldings? And does he eat properly? But, of course, you've seen him; you know what he's like. He really is wonderful with his hands: he was always like that, even as a boy, when a faucet leaked, or something went wrong with the Singer, or the radio was all static, he could fix anything in a minute. But there's another side to it: I mean, when he was studying he always had to have something in his hands, to take apart and put back together, and as you know, taking apart is easy, and putting back together isn't. But then he learned, and he didn't cause any more damage."

I could see them with my mind's eye, Faussone's hands: long, solid, and quick, much more expressive than his face.

They illustrated and glossed his tales, imitating, as required, a shovel, a monkey wrench, a hammer. In the stagnant air of the mess hall they designed the elegant catenaries of the suspension bridge and the spires of the derricks, coming to the rescue of speech when it stalled. They had reminded me of distant readings of Darwin, of the artificer's hand that, making tools and bending matter, stirred the human brain from its torpor and still guides and stimulates and draws it ahead, as a dog does with a blind master.

"For us he's like a son. Imagine! He lived in this house for eight years, and even now—"

"Seven. Not eight," Mentina corrected, with inexplicable harshness, not looking at me.

Teresa continued, unheeding: "—and we must say that he was very little trouble, at least while he stayed at Lancia, as long as he led a somewhat regular life, that is. Now, of course, he makes more; but I ask you: can a man go on that way for his whole life? Like a bird on the branch, here today and tomorrow heaven knows where. Baking in the desert one minute and buried in snow the next. To say nothing of the hard work. . . ."

". . . and the danger. Working high up on those towers makes my head swim just to think about it," Mentina added, as if she were reproaching her sister, holding her responsible.

"I hope that, as the years go by, he'll calm down a bit, but for the present it seems impossible. You should see him when he's in Turin. After two or three days, he's like a caged lion. Here in the house we hardly see him, and I suspect sometimes he goes straight to a pensione and doesn't get in touch with the two of us. One thing's certain: healthy as he is, if he keeps on like this, he'll still ruin his stomach. When he's here with us, there's no getting him to come home and eat at regular hours, peacefully seated at the table, putting something hot and nourishing inside him. It's like he's sitting on nails: a roll, a piece of cheese, and he's off! And he comes back late at night when the two of us are already asleep, because we go to bed early."

"And for us, too, cooking something special for him would

be such a pleasure, because just for ourselves it's not worth the trouble. And he's our only nephew, and we have all the time in the world. . . ."

By now the procedure had been established, not without some uneasiness on my part. Teresa looked at me when she spoke; Mentina added her remarks, while looking at Teresa; and I sat and listened, keeping my eye chiefly on Mentina. And i perceived in her an acrimony hard to define. I couldn't understand whether it was directed at me or at her sister, or at the distant nephew or at his fate, which, after all, didn't seem particularly deserving of commiseration. In the two sisters I was recognizing an example of that divergence and polarization often to be observed in couples, not necessarily husband and wife. At the beginning of their living together, the differences may be slight between the instinctively generous partner and the stingy one, between the tidy and the untidy, the sedentary and the rover, the talkative and the taciturn. But as the years go by, those differences become accentuated and turn into precise specializations. In some cases it may be a rejection of direct competition, so that when one of the pair shows signs of dominating in a given field, the other, instead of fighting on that ground, chooses another area, adjacent or remote. In other cases, one of the couple may seek, consciously or not, to compensate with his own behavior the deficiencies of the other, as when the wife of a contemplative or lazy man is forced to take an active interest in practical matters. A similar differentiation has developed in many animal species, where, for example, the male is exclusively a hunter and the female attends only to rearing the offspring. In the same way Aunt Teresa had become specialized in contacts with the outside world, and Aunt Mentina had shut herself up in the house. One dealt with foreign affairs and one with the interior, obviously not without zones of envy, friction, and reciprocal criticism.

I tried to reassure the two ladies: "No, you mustn't worry about his eating. I've seen how Tino lives. When he's on a job, he has to follow a schedule, like it or not, no matter what country he may be in. And another thing: the farther you go from civilized countries, the more you can be sure of eating healthful food, unfamiliar, perhaps, but healthful; so he won't ruin his stomach. For that matter, from what I can see, Tino enjoys enviable health. Isn't that true?"

"Oh, yes, that's true," Mentina spoke up. "He's never sick, always fine. He never needs anything. He doesn't need anybody." Poor Aunt Mentina was downright transparent; she, after all, did need somebody, a person who would need her: Tino, in other words.

Aunt Teresa offered me a liqueur and some macaroons and asked my leave to open the package I had brought from Russia. It contained two fur collars, one white and one brown. I'm no expert, but I had the impression they weren't particularly prized furs, probably bought in the Beriozhka stores, a virtually obligatory stop for the tourist who pays a three-day visit to Moscow.

"Aren't they wonderful! And it was very kind of you to bring them all the way here. We're sorry you were put to such trouble; you could have telephoned, and we would have come to get them. Heaven only knows how much they cost him, poor boy, and for us, really, they're too grand. Maybe he thinks we still go strolling along Via Roma. Well, why not? This would be a good excuse to get back into that habit, eh, Mentina? We're not yet decrepit, after all."

"He doesn't talk much, Tino doesn't; but he has his feelings. He takes after his mother. To look at, he seems just a rough country boy, but that's only appearances."

I nodded politely, but I knew I was lying. It wasn't only appearances, Faussone's rough nature; maybe he hadn't been born that way and maybe he had once been different, but by now that character was real, ingrained, reinforced by countless duels with his adversary, hard by definition: the iron of his structures and his bolts, the adversary that never forgives your mistakes and often extends them into blame. He was different, the man I had come to know, from the figure that the two good aunts ("one is smart, the other not so smart") had constructed and made the object of their love, so tepidly requited. Their retreat-hermitage of Via Lagrange, immune to the passage of decades, suitably represented by the *causeuse* in which I was seated, was a bad observatory. Even if Faussone had agreed to talk a bit more, he would in no way have been able to bring to life, amid these draperies, his defeats and his victories, his fears and his inventions.

"What Tino needs," Teresa said, "is a nice girl. Don't you agree? We've thought about it heaven knows how many times, and we even tried, over and over again. And it would seem easy, because he's a good boy, too, a hard worker, nice-looking. He has no bad habits and makes good money. But would you believe it? We introduce them; they see each other, go out two or three times; and then the girl comes here and bursts into tears: it's all over. And there's no understanding what happened. He, needless to say, never utters a word. And as for the girls, each of them tells a different story: that he's a bear, that he made her walk four miles without saying a word, that he gives himself airs. A disaster, in other words, and now everybody knows; there's been talk, and we don't dare arrange any more meetings for him. And yet, he may not think about his future, but we do, because we're some years older than he is, and we know what it's like to live alone. And we also know that to live with somebody, you have to have a fixed residence. Otherwise, you actually do end up a bear. You meet so many of them, on Sundays especially, and you recognize them at once. And every time I see one, I think of Tino and it makes me sad. But you—maybe one evening when you're talking about personal matters—couldn't you say a word to him?"

I promised I would, and again I knew I was lying. I wouldn't say a word to him; I wouldn't give him advice; I wouldn't attempt in any way to influence him, to contribute to the construction of a future for him, to deflect the future he was constructing himself, or his fate. Only an obscure, carnal, ancient love, like the love of his aunts, could presume to know what effects would spring from the causes, what metamorphosis the rigger Tino Faussone would undergo if bound to one woman and a "fixed residence." It is already difficult for a chemist to foresee, beyond his experience, the interaction between two simple molecules: quite impossible to predict what will happen at the encounter of two slightly complex molecules. How to predict the results of an encounter between two human beings? Or the reactions of an individual dealing with a new situation? Nothing can be said: nothing sure, nothing probable, nothing honest. Better to err through omission than through commission: better to refrain from steering the fate of others, since it is already so difficult to navigate one's own.

It wasn't easy for me to take my leave of the two ladies. They kept finding new subjects of conversation, and they maneuvered to forestall me whenever I sought to clear a path toward the front door. The rumble of a commercial jet was heard, and from the window of the breakfast nook, against the now-dark sky, the throb of its lights could be seen.

"Every time one goes by I think of him, and how he isn't afraid of crashing," Aunt Teresa said. "And imagine! We've never even been in Milan, and to Genoa only once, to see the sea!"

ANCHOVIES II

THEY'RE ALL RIGHT, that pair, no doubt about it. But every now and then they kind of get on your back. Thanks for delivering the package. I hope you didn't have to waste too much time. So you're leaving on Tuesday, too? With the *samolyot?* Good, we can make the trip together. As far as Moscow anyway it's the same route."

It was a long and complicated route, and I was happy to be able to travel for some of the way in company, not least because Faussone, who had made the trip many times, knew it better than I did, and especially he knew the ropes better. I was also pleased because my battle against the anchovies had ended substantially in my favor.

It was drizzling. According to the plans, a factory car would be waiting for us in front of the building, to take us to the airport, about forty kilometers away. Eight o'clock went by, then eight-thirty. The ground was all mud, and there was nobody to be seen. Around nine a pickup truck arrived. The driver got out and asked us, "Are there three of you?"

"No, two of us," Faussone replied.

"French?"

"No, Italian."

"Are you going to the station?"

"No, we're going to the airport."

The driver, a herculean young man with a radiant face, concluded, paradoxically: "In that case, get in." He loaded our luggage on board and set off. The road was interrupted by vast mud puddles; he must have known it well, because he plunged straight into some of them without slowing down, while he cautiously skirted others.

"I'm glad, too," Faussone said to me, "first because I was beginning to get a bit fed up with these parts; second, because that excavator back there, that animal with legs . . . it meant a lot to me, and now I've seen it finished. It isn't in operation yet, but I've left it in good hands. And your business? Those cans for fish: how did it go?"

"It went well. In the end we proved right, but it wasn't a nice story. No, it was rather a stupid story, not one of those stories it's a pleasure to tell, because, in telling it, I have to recall how stupid I was, not to figure things out earlier."

"Don't take it to heart," Faussone replied. "On jobs, almost all stories end like that: all stories, really, where it's a matter of figuring things out. The same thing happens when you finish reading a murder mystery, and you slap your forehead and say 'Of course!', but it's only an impression. The fact is that in real life things are never that simple. Only the problems they make you do in school are simple. Well then?"

"Well then, I stayed in Turin for over a month. I ran all the checks again, and I came back here convinced I had a hand full of trumps. But I found that the Russians were convinced the trumps were in their hands: they had examined several dozen drums, and according to them at least one drum out of every five was defective; that is, it produced gritty tests. And one thing was certain: all the gritty samples—and only they— couldn't withstand the anchovies. The technician treated me with that short temper people have with fools. He, personally, had made a discovery—"

"Beware of clients who make discoveries: they're worse than mules."

"No, no. He had discovered something very serious from

my point of view. As you know, I was convinced there was some local factor: I suspected the grittiness came from the little metal strips used for the tests, or from the brushes they spread the enamel with. He had me up against the ropes; he had found a way to prove that the lumps existed already in the enamel. He took the viscometer—it's not a complicated instrument: it's a cylindrical cup with a conic base, which ends in a calibrated nozzle. You cover the nozzle with one finger, fill the cup with enamel, let the air bubbles come to the surface; then you remove your finger and press a stopwatch at the same time. You measure the viscosity by the time it takes for the cup to empty. It's an important test, because the viscosity of a paint shouldn't alter during storage.

"Well, this technician had discovered that you could tell which drums were defective even without smearing the enamel on the test strips. You just had to observe carefully the trickle of paint from the nozzle of the viscometer; if the drum was good, the flow was steady and smooth as glass; if the drum was bad, the flow had breaks, jerks: three or four, or even five, for every cup. So there were lumps already in the enamel, he said. And I felt like Christ on the cross, and I told him that they couldn't be observed any other way; the enamel looked nice and clear, before the measuring and afterwards."

Faussone interrupted: "Excuse me, but it sounds to me like he was right. If a thing can be seen, that's a sign it exists."

"Of course, but you know the old saying: error is such an ugly animal, nobody wants him in the house. When I saw that little golden trickle flowing in fits and starts, as if it wanted to mock me, I felt the blood rush to my head, and my mind was a whirl of confused ideas. On the one hand, I thought of the tests I had made in Turin, that had all gone well. On the other hand, I thought that an enamel is a much more complicated thing than anyone imagines. Some engineer friends of mine have told me it's difficult even to be sure what a brick or a coil spring will do over a period of time. Well, believe me, I've had many years of experience, and paints resemble us more than they do bricks. They're born, they grow old, and they die like us; and when they're old, they can turn foolish, and even when they're young, they can deceive you, and they're actually capable of telling lies, pretending to be what they aren't: to be sick when they're healthy, and healthy when they're sick. It's easy to say the same causes should produce the same effects: this is an invention of people who have things done, instead of doing things themselves. Try talking about it with a farmer, or a schoolteacher, or a doctor, or, most of all, a politician. If they're honest and intelligent, they'll burst out laughing."

Suddenly we were flung upward and banged our heads against the roof of the vehicle. The driver had come to a closed railway crossing and had swerved abruptly to the right, running obliquely into a ditch, then off the road; now he was driving parallel to the tracks over a plowed field. He turned proudly to us, not to see if we were intact, but to shout something I didn't understand.

"He says it's quicker this way," Faussone translated, with a rather unconvinced look. A little later, the driver boldly showed us another closed crossing and made a gesture as if to say, You see? And he dashed up an embankment, regaining the road. "That's the Russians for you," Faussone murmured to me, "either boring or crazy. Thank God the airport's near."

"My Russian, the technician, was neither crazy nor boring: he was like me, a man playing his part and trying to do his duty. He was just a bit too enamored of his viscometer discovery, but I have to admit that, during these past days, I didn't feel up to loving him the way the Bible wants us to. I had to have time to get my thoughts straight, and I asked him to allow me a complete test program. By now all three thousand drums of our shipment were in their warehouses, numbered progressively. I asked to recheck them, in my defense: at least one out of three, if not all of them. It was a stupid, long task (and, in fact, it took me two weeks), but I couldn't see any other solution.

"We prepared strips eight hours a day, hundreds of them; the gritty ones we didn't even test. We put the smooth ones at night under the anchovies: they all held up. After four or five days' work, I thought I could see a certain regularity, but I couldn't explain it, and by itself it didn't explain anything: there seemed to be good days and bad days, I mean: smooth days and gritty days. But it wasn't clear-cut: on the smooth days there were always some gritty samples, and on the gritty days a fair number of smooth samples."

We came to the airport; our driver waved goodbye; turned the vehicle around with a loud squeal of tires, as if he were in an exceptional hurry; and darted away again in a flash. His eyes following the truck as it flew off between two curtains of mud, Faussone grumbled: "The mother of fools is always pregnant, even in this country." Then he turned to me: "Sorry, wait a minute before you tell the rest. I'm interested, but we have to go through customs. I'm interested, because one time I was dealing with a crane that would stall on some days and not stall on other days. But then we figured it out; it wasn't anything unusual. Only the dampness."

We got into the customs line, but a little middle-aged woman promptly arrived, who spoke English fairly well, and she led us to the head of the line without anyone's protesting. I was amazed, but Faussone explained that they had recognized us as foreigners; maybe the factory had telephoned about us. We went through in an instant; we could have exported a machine gun or a kilo of heroin. The customs inspector only asked me if I had any books; I had one, in English, about the life of dolphins, and he was puzzled and asked me why I had it, where I had bought it, if I was English, and was I an expert on fish? I wasn't? Then how did I happen to have this book, and why did I want to take it to Italy? Having heard my answers, he consulted a superior, then let me pass.

The plane was already on the tarmac, and the seats were nearly all occupied; it was a little turboprop, and its interior had a homey look. There were whole families, obviously peasants: babies asleep in their mother's arms, baskets of fruit and vegetables more or less everywhere, in one corner, three live chickens, their legs tied together. There was no partition (or it had been removed) between the pilot's cabin and the passengers' space; the two pilots, waiting to receive the clearance signal, munched sunflower seeds and chatted with the hostess and (via radio) with somebody in the control tower. The hostess was a pretty girl, very young, sturdy, and pale. She wasn't in uniform, but was wearing a little black dress and a violet shawl carelessly thrown around her shoulders. After a while she glanced at her wristwatch, came out among the passengers, and greeted two or three acquaintances. She told us her name was Vyera Filippovna and she was our hostess. She spoke in a mild voice and a familiar tone, without that mechanical emphasis hostesses always use. She then went on to say that we would be leaving in a few minutes or perhaps half an hour, and the flight would last an hour and a half or maybe two hours. Would we please fasten our seat belts and not smoke until takeoff? From her bag she took a bundle of long transparent plastic envelopes and said: "If anyone has a fountain pen, please put it in one of these bags."

"Why?" a passenger asked. "Isn't the plane pressurized?"

"Yes, it's somewhat pressurized, citizen, but take my advice all the same. For that matter, fountain pens leak even on the ground, as everybody knows."

The plane took off, and I resumed my story.

"As I was telling you, there were, roughly speaking, good days and bad days. And, also roughly speaking, the tests made in the morning were worse than those made in the afternoon. I spent my days making tests and my evenings thinking about them, and I couldn't make head or tail of it. When they telephoned me from Turin to find out how things were progressing, I would turn red with shame. I made promises, I stalled for time, and I felt as if I were rowing in a boat tied to a pole, breaking my back and getting nowhere. I thought about it in the evening, and into the night, because I couldn't sleep. Every now and then I would turn on the lamp and start reading the dolphin book, to make the hours pass.

"One night, instead of reading the book, I began rereading my diary. It wasn't really a diary, just some notes I jotted down, day by day; it's a habit that anyone who does a fairly complicated job falls into, especially as the years pass and you can't trust your memory so much any more. To avoid arousing suspicions, I didn't write anything during the day, but I would scribble my notes and my observations in the evening, as soon as I got back to the dormitory—which, by the way, was terribly depressing. Well, rereading them was even more depressing, because no sense emerged. There was only a regularity, but it could be just coincidence; the worst days were the ones when Kondratova turned up. That's right: the woman whose husband and sons had been killed in the war, you remember? Maybe it was the misfortune she had undergone, but the fact is that the poor thing didn't get on my nerves only; she upset everybody. I had made a note of the days when she came because of that visa question; she was handling it, or rather she should have been handling it, but instead she told me about her past woes and made me lose time on the job. She also teased me about the anchovies. I don't think she was spiteful; perhaps she didn't realize I was being held personally responsible, but certainly she wasn't a woman you were glad to have around. In any case, I don't believe in the evil eye, and I couldn't accept the idea that Kondratova's misfortunes could turn into lumps in the enamel. For that matter, she never touched anything with her hands; she didn't come every day, but when she did, she arrived early, and the first thing she did was berate all the lab people because, in her opinion, the place wasn't clean enough.

"Yes, it was the cleaning that put me on the right track. The old saying 'Night brings counsel' is rather true, but it brings counsel only to those who can't sleep, with a mind that never takes time off and keeps churning. That night I felt as if I were at the movies and they were showing a bad film—not only bad, it was also a poor print, and every moment or so it would break, then start over again; and the first person to appear was, in fact, Kondratova. She entered the laboratory, greeted me, preached her usual sermon about cleanliness; then the film broke. What happened next? Well, after I don't know how many interruptions, the sequences continued for a few more frames, and the woman was seen sending one of the girls off for some rags. The rags were seen in close up, and instead of rags, some were of a broad-meshed white material like hospital gauze. You know how these things happen: it wasn't a miraculous dream, I probably had seen it happen in reality, but perhaps I was distracted at that moment, thinking of other things, or Kondratova may have been telling me the story of Leningrad and the siege. I must have recorded the memory unaware.

"The next morning Kondratova wasn't there. I acted casual, as if nothing particular was on my mind. And I went to poke my nose in the box of rags. With sign language, insistence, and intuition, from the explanations of the technician, I learned this was material for bandages that had been rejected during testing. Obviously, the man was playing dumb, exploiting the language barrier. It didn't take me long to realize that the gauze had been obtained illegally, perhaps through barter or thanks to some friendships. Perhaps the monthly allotment of rags hadn't turned up or was late, and he had made do on his own—all for the best motives, of course.

"That day it was sunny, the first sunshine after a week of cloudy skies. Honestly, I think that if the sun had come out earlier I would have understood before the business of the gritty tests. I took a rag from the box, I shook it two or three times; a moment later, at the opposite end of the laboratory, an almost invisible ray of sunlight filled with luminous particles, blinking on and off like fireflies in May. Now I must tell you (perhaps I've told you already) that paints are a touchy family, especially as far as hairs are concerned, or anything that flies through the air. A colleague of mine had to pay a lot of money to a landowner, to make him cut down a row of poplars six hundred meters from the factory; otherwise in May those tufts, with seeds inside, that are so pretty and fly so far, would end up in the batches of paint being milled and would ruin them. And mosquito nets and screens were no use at all, because the tufts came in through all the fissures of the window and door frames, collected at night in corners; and in the morning, as soon as the ventilators were turned on, they whirled furiously in the air.

"And I once got into trouble thanks to fruit flies. I don't know if you're familiar with the species, but scientists love them because they have very big chromosomes. In fact, it seems that almost everything we know today about heredity biologists learned thanks to these insects, crossbreeding them in every possible way, cutting them up, injecting stuff into them, starving them, giving them strange things to eat. So you see, showing off can frequently be dangerous. They were given the name *Drosophila*, and they are also beautiful, with red eyes, at most three millimeters long, and they don't do anyone any harm. On the contrary, maybe against their will, they've done us good.

"These little creatures love vinegar; I couldn't tell you why. To be specific, they love the acetic acid that's in vinegar. They pick up its odor at incredible distances, they gather from all sides like a cloud, on must, for example, which does actually contain some traces of acetic acid. And if they find real vinegar, they act drunk; they fly around and around it in a dense circle, and often they fall in and drown."

"If you keep putting your hand in the honey pot, you're sure to get stung," Faussone remarked, quoting yet another proverb.

"When I talk about them smelling, that's just a figure of speech . . . they don't have noses, of course; they perceive smells with their antennae. But when it does come to smelling, if I can call it that, they're way ahead of us and even ahead of dogs, because they sense the acid in a compound, for example, in ethyl or butyl acetate, which are solvents of nitrocellulose lacquers. Well, we had a nitrocellulose fingernail polish, a very special color; we spent two days adjusting the color and were passing it through the three-roll mill. I couldn't tell you why— maybe it was their season, or maybe they were hungrier than usual, or else they had spread the word—but they came in swarms, lighted on the rolls as they turned, and got ground into the lacquer. We realized it only at the end of the process, and there was no way of filtering. Rather than throw the stuff away, we added it to some antirust paint, and it came out a nice rosé shade. Sorry if I've strayed from the subject.

"To conclude: at this point I felt I was back on the track. I expounded to the technician my supposition, that was secretly almost a certitude, so much so that I was going to ask permission to telephone the news to the factory in Italy. But the technician wouldn't give in: with his own eyes he had seen various samples of enamel, barely taken from the drums, that came through the viscometer in fits and starts. How would they have had time to catch the threads of the rags in the air? For him it was clear: the threads might or might not have something to do with it, but the lumps were already there, in the drums, when they came in.

"I had to show him (and also myself) that it wasn't true, and that every lump contained a thread from the gauze. Did they have a microscope? They did: a student instrument with only two hundred magnifications, but that was enough for what I wanted to do. It also had a polarizer and an analyzer."

Faussone interrupted me: "Hold it a minute. While I was telling you stories about my job, you have to admit, I never took advantage. I know you're all pleased with yourself now, but you mustn't take advantage, either. You have to tell things so people can understand; otherwise the game's over. Or are you already on the other side: one of those people who write and then the reader has to fend for himself since he's already paid for the book anyway?"

He was right; I had been carried away. On the other hand, I was in a hurry to end my story, because Vyera Filippovna was already moving along the aisle to announce that, in her opinion, we would be landing in Moscow in twenty or thirty minutes. So I simply explained to him that there are long molecules and short molecules; that only long molecules, whether in nature or man-made, manage to produce strong filaments; that in these filaments, these threads of wool or cotton or nylon or silk or whatever, the molecules are oriented lengthwise and are roughly parallel; and that the polarizer and the analyzer are instruments that allow us to perceive this parallelism, even on a fragment of a filament barely visible under the microscope. If the molecules are oriented, if it's a thread, in other words, you see beautiful colors; if they are jumbled at random, you don't see anything. Faussone grunted, to indicate that I could continue.

"In a drawer I also found some beautiful little glass spoons, the kind used for precision weighing. I wanted to show the technician that in every lump that came from the viscometer there was a filament, and that where there were no filaments there were also no lumps. I had the place thoroughly cleaned with wet rags, I made them remove the rag box, and that afternoon I began my hunt: I had to catch the lump with the spoon as it came down from the viscometer and then take it to the microscope. I think it could become a sport, a kind of skeet shooting you can also do at home. But it was no fun practicing the sport while four or five pairs of suspicious eyes were watching me. For ten or twenty minutes I didn't get anywhere. I was always there too late, after the lump had passed. Or else, driven by nerves, I would stick the spoon under an imaginary lump. Then I learned that the important thing was to be comfortably seated, under a strong light, holding the spoon very close to the flow of paint. I succeeded in capturing a first lump and put it under the microscope, and the filament was there. I compared it with another filament I had removed from the gauze for this purpose. Perfect: they were identical, both cotton.

"The next day—yesterday, that is—I developed a real skill and also taught one of the girls to do the trick. There were no more doubts: every lump contained a filament. And the filaments then acted as a fifth column for the anchovies' attack on the enamel. This was fairly easily explained, because cotton fibers are porous, and they could easily serve as a conduit. But the Russians didn't ask me anything further; they signed my protocol of absolution and sent me off with a new order for enamel in my pocket. By the way, even without knowing much Russian, I realized that, with one excuse or another, they would have given me the order in any case, because the German enamel that Kondratova had told me about the previous month, obviously, when it came to lumps and anchovies, behaved just like ours. And the technician's discovery, the thing that had worried me so, proved to have a downright ridiculous cause: between one test and the next, instead of washing the viscometer with solvent and then drying it, they cleansed it directly with gauze rags from the box, so that, when it came to lumps, the viscometer itself was the worst hotbed of infection."

We landed in Moscow, reclaimed our luggage, and got into the bus that was to take us to our hotel in the city. I was rather disappointed at the results of my attempt to meet Faussone on his own ground; he had followed my story with his usual inexpressive face, almost without interrupting me and without asking questions. But he must have been pursuing a private train of thought, because after a long silence he said to me: "So you really want to shut up shop? Excuse me for saying so, but if I was in your shoes, I'd give it some careful thought. I tell you, doing things you can touch with your hands has an advantage: you can make comparisons and understand how much you're worth. You make a mistake, you correct it, and next time you don't make it. But you're older than me, and maybe you've already seen enough things in your life."

What was needed of course was Captain MacWhirr. Directly I perceived him I could see that he was the man for the situation. I don't mean to say that I ever saw Captain MacWhirr in the flesh, or had ever come in contact with his literal mind and his dauntless temperament. MacWhirr is not an acquaintance of a few hours, or a few weeks, or a few months. He is the product of twenty years of life. My own life. Conscious invention had little to do with him. If it is true that Captain MacWhirr never walked and breathed on this earth (which I find for my part extremely difficult to believe) I can also assure my readers that he is perfectly authentic.

—Joseph Conrad, Author's Note to *Typhoon*

With this quotation I would like to tell the reader that, just as Conrad never saw Captain MacWhirr "in the flesh," so I never actually met Libertino Faussone. Like the British captain, Faussone is imaginary but "perfectly authentic," at the same time; he is a compound, a mosaic of numerous men I have met, similar to Faussone and similar among themselves, in personality, virtue, individuality, and in their view of work and the world.

—P. L.